NEVER - BROKEN Blood Line

The Rosenthal family – Book II

By: Leesa Payne Fort

Copyright © 2024 Leesa Payne Fort
All rights reserved.

Other titles by author:
Dr. Taylor and the Stork
Forever – Always (Blood love)
The Pits – Where the snakes don't hiss

TABLE OF CONTENTS

CH. 01   pg. 1
CH. 02   pg. 6
CH. 03   pg. 10
CH. 04   pg. 12
CH. 05   pg. 16
CH. 06   pg. 19
CH. 07   pg. 23
CH. 08   pg. 27
CH. 09   pg. 33
CH. 10   pg. 39
CH. 11   pg. 41
CH. 12   pg. 44
CH. 13   pg. 50
CH. 14   pg. 52
CH. 15   pg. 56
CH. 16   pg. 61
CH. 17   pg. 67
CH. 18   pg. 69
CH. 19   pg. 71
CH. 20   pg. 74
CH. 21   pg. 77
CH. 22   pg. 80
CH. 23   pg. 83
CH. 24   pg. 85
CH. 25   pg. 88
CH. 26   pg. 92
CH. 27   pg. 98
CH. 28   pg. 101
CH. 29   pg. 107
CH. 30   pg. 110

PROLOGUE

Today is February the first and I am now Mrs. Cam Rosenthal. I look at everything before this day as a journey that I somehow managed to live through. A long road that made me stronger, that gave me courage, that taught me to believe in others where, as before, I couldn't.

I reminisced frequently about the day I shot Charles. I had questions that have now been answered, leading me to know more about the man my mother loved.

Rayan is the one who saved Charles that day, he was able to do so because Charles wasn't immortal. I trusted his existence because of the things I chose to hear. A young girl's mind can become entangled in love very quickly, leaving so much else to the imagination, delusional in a sense.

As I screamed for Cam to help Charles while he lay with his brains spilling out, Rayan had already done so by pouring his blood into Charles. Charles was only immortal for the last moments of his life.

They coaxed me into feeding Charles my blood as a test of my loyalty. I failed miserably.

Cam killed Charles by beheading him in my presence so I would learn a hard lesson - I should never share what belongs to Cam.

I no longer feel remorse for my actions that day, Cam took my sadness away. I often wondered if Charles were now part of the training camp along with my father, but I somehow doubted it, simply because Cam's jealousy over me ran deeper than his very being. I loved that about him.

Cam and I boarded Wesley's jet once again and headed out on our spectacular honeymoon. We had chosen the Island of Bermuda simply so we could explore the Crystal and Fantasy Caves - Perfect for Cam, an exciting underworld for us both.

Fate brought us together but something bigger than that would keep us united.

We lived a good life, an unexpected life. I was so much more now than I ever imagined I could be. The surrealness of marriage and travel was just the beginning.

CHAPTER 1

"Doctor, doctor, my wife is in labor." I heard that so often while visiting the Children's Research Hospital in Memphis.

Cam and I walked down the long corridor trying to make our way to the conference room we had been instructed to meet in.

That man was so excited about his little bundle of joy about to make an entrance into this world, that he yelled out for anyone in a white coat to assist them. A nurse finally escorted the couple down to the Emergency Department. Cam looked at me and smiled as an indication that one day that would be us. I flashed a grin back, but with unnoticed doubt. This wonderful man, that I now call my husband has always promised me the world as if he could give it to me. I still desired and loved everything about him. Through all my heartache, I looked to him for security and peace. He has yet to fail me. He was my everything, especially now with my mother gone.

This was my first trip of many to Memphis and to this hospital that I cannot put an adjective to, simply because it is a place where sick kids are looked after and treated.

Once we made our way down the seemingly endless hall, Cam opened the conference room door flashing his admiring eyes in my direction as he guided me to the table, pulling out the chair he wished for me to sit in. A widely respected gentleman he was, indeed.

I wore a black pant suit with a matching jacket over top a silk blouse, rarely did I leave home without the platinum tree necklace Cam gave to me on the first day of high school back in Rhode Island. That same day he gifted me a Mercedes Benz to get me to and from school safely. I had many pieces of jewelry now - some more valuable than people could imagine. Jewelry so magnificent, the pieces were sure to become heirlooms. But, to whom - I didn't know. That would depend upon my decisions in the future and whether I would choose to become immortal. I was in no rush to decide anything.

I have matured greatly since our marriage. The ways of the world were thrust at me but with the understanding that its cruelness could never hurt me or the ones I love.

I glanced around the enormous table to familiarize myself with the other faces in the room. Wesley's daughter Sharon and her husband Ken were there. She quickly noticed Cam and hurried over to plant a kiss on his cheek.

"Cam, darling!" Her loud obnoxious tone pierced my ears.

Cam awkwardly smiled.

"Hello Millie, how have you been?" Sharon looked down at me, running her fingers through her hair.

Cam quickly corrected her. "Her name is Marry. I believe you are aware of that." His mouth tightly closed.

"Oh dear, you know how bad I am with names." Her arrogant response didn't help matters.

He nodded and stared blankly at her until she made her way back to the other side of the room. Her friendliness to him was uncalled for, add the blatant disrespect she showed me, the result gave me a feeling of panic.

I placed my hands in my lap and fidgeted with my diamond wedding ring, much larger than anyone else's in the place. I glanced up to find Sharon's husband Ken focused on me. He ran his tongue across his mouth, appearing just as evil as her.

Trying to fight off the anxiety, I excused myself and journeyed around until I came across a water fountain. I pulled my hair back and held it in a makeshift ponytail letting the cool water run down my lips. The feeling relaxed me.

The buzzing, bright lights had carried me further away than I suspected, unable to find my way back. I looked around, lost.

"You're so pretty." Startled by a young girl in a wheelchair, I turned and bent down to hug her.

"You, my dear, are much prettier than I." My heart ached for the youth.

"Are you sick, too?" She asked.

"No, sweetheart. I'm here with my husband for a meeting. I seem to have gotten a little turned around and am unsure where I came from." I giggled as did she.

"Over there." She pointed. "I noticed you as soon as you came out of the room."

It wasn't very far at all. The room was engulfed in glass windows, so it didn't take me long to recognize where I belonged. Neither did any amount of time lapse before I took notice of Sharon's new position in my seat, next to Cam. The two laughed, seemingly having the time of their lives. I didn't take their carrying on lightly. Cam hadn't realized I was back, so I left, thanking my new friend for her help, and wishing her well. Juan drove me back to the hotel.

I second guessed my exit, but I couldn't sit back and be disrespected especially after watching my fairly young mother die of early onset Alzheimer's - Seeing the way she was spoken too and looked down upon at times changed me as a person.

Juan escorted me up the room, knowing that should anything happen to me, he would have to deal with Cam. He didn't want that.

"Mrs. Rosenthal." I stopped him at the beginning of his sentence.

"Mrs. Rosenthal is my grandmother, just call me Marry." I said.

"Mrs. Marry, is there anything else I can assist you with?" He asked.

He was very polite and a blessing to have on my team. "Well Juan, there is just one thing if you don't mind. When you pick up Cam and are headed back this way, will you please notify me before your arrival? He agreed. I was anxious to deal with Cam's feelings about my departure.

A couple of hours passed before I heard from Juan. I paced the floor, preparing myself for Cam's response to my actions.

The door flung open, ricocheting off the back wall. I jumped, startled by the harsh noise it made. "Oh, how nice, you have your little fangs out and everything!" I snipped. "Do you plan to use those things on someone, dear?" I asked, wanting to refer to Sharon but realizing that would be too much.

He angrily swept me into his arms, in the midst of ripping his shirt off, he placed me down gently on the sofa. Trying to intimidate me, he let out an ugly growl. He pushed my head to the side, sinking his teeth into my neck, he drank of me. Aware of his limitations, he abruptly stopped, frantically rising back to his feet, blood dripping everywhere. He then walked out of the room.

I thought about chasing after him, realizing his anger but I didn't do anything wrong. This was all on him. I fell asleep on the couch leaving him to sulk alone in the bedroom.

I awoke quickly around three a.m. My eyes popped open to Cam standing above me, panting heavily. His mouth quivered as he tried to produce a smile. He bent down, picked me up and carried me back to the bedroom. He climbed in the bed next to me and watched my every breath.

"What is going on with you, Marry, leaving without my consent? I was very concerned when I could not find you. Had Juan not told me of your where abouts, bad things could have transpired."

I found his claim of worry quite absurd.

"You made me promise that I would never walk out on you, but you turn around and do exactly that to me. Why?"

He asked.

I contemplated telling him about Ken and his obnoxiousness, but I decided against that seeing as I was in the middle of a panic attack, I could have quite possibly imagined such. I did however feel compelled to disclose my disapproval of his behavior with Sharon.

"When I came back from the water fountain, it made me ill to see Sharon had placed herself in my chair. The two of you were giggling and chatting up a storm, how dare me to disrupt such fun!" I neared a yell.

"You're telling me that you were jealous of me having a conversation with Sharon? Wesley's daughter, Sharon?" He asked.

"Yep, the Sharon that called me Millie! That one, Cam!" How could he not see how inconsiderate he had been.

"Marry, get up, you and I are going to take a walk." He took my arm insisting I budge.

"At this time of morning?" Three a.m. wasn't a very pleasant time to walk around Memphis and the temperatures were extremely frigid for this time of year. We both put on our black leather trench coats and headed out of the hotel. There was only a hand full of people in the lobby, their eyes focused on the two of us and our crazy midmorning outing.

I snuggled underneath his arm, shielding myself from the wind as we made our way down Danny Thomas Place and back into the hospital I chose to abandon earlier.

"Why are we here?" I asked.

He took me by the hand and hurried us through the Emergency Room entrance. It was the only way in after dark. Every hospital employee in our path greeted Cam by name and smiled lovingly at me as if I were accompanied by some sort of hero on a mission.

The ding from the elevator prompted us to take a few steps back allowing its occupants to unload. Alone, we boarded the metal box. The number six lit up when Cam pressed the button giving a hint to our destination. I knew the floor number now but was still unsure of why we were here. The music was boring, a dull instrumental. We both looked up towards the bright lights with nothing to say to one another.

The sixth-floor nurses' station was nothing different than downstairs. Hellos came from every direction. "Hello, Mr. Rosenthal – Hey, Cam." Their friendliness disgusted me. My jealousy ran just as deep as his.

"Is this the wife?" An orderly cleaning up a spill outside of one the rooms questioned. Cam properly introduced me to the man; I gave him a half smile.

We travelled down a long dark hallway, entering the last patient room that stood alone where normally you would find more. An oddity.

The curtain was pulled, the lights were out but the television gave off enough glow to see around the place.

"Be very quiet." Cam put his finger up to his mouth.

We tip-toed up to the partition. He gently pulled it back so that we could both see in. I loudly gasped causing whatever it was to move. The thing rolled over and looked at us.

"Uncle Cam." It spoke.

"Hey buddy, I was just coming by to check on you. I didn't mean to wake you. Go back to sleep." Cam's whisper was sympathetic and sweet.

He turned on a small light positioned at the top of his bed. It was definitely a male and not as distorted as I originally thought. I was ashamed of the way I had been thinking lately, my once open mind was now a bit judgmental, and I didn't like that about myself.

I guess the boy wanted to see me as much as I wanted to get a good look at him.

"Who is that with you, Uncle Cam?" He asked.

"This is my wife, Marry, remember the one I was telling you about?" Cam moved closer to the bed.

"Awwh, yeah, I remember." His little voice was raspy. He appeared to be about seven if he was indeed human.

"Hi, Marry." He reached his hand out to me. I softly wrapped mine around his.

"Hello there, sir. I didn't catch your name." Cam took a few steps back and shockingly let the child answer for himself.

"I'm Skylar. Nice to meet you, Marry." He was polite and the more he spoke, the more he revealed his identity. He was just a child, a kid was the only proper way to view him.

"Likewise." I patted him before releasing my hold.

The toilet flushed, alarming me to someone else's presence. Cam nodded to let me know everything was okay. A man or possibly vampire stepped out of the restroom. I never really knew the genetic makeup of those who were around me anymore.

"What's up Cam?" He shook Cam's hand while slyly looking me up and down.

"Mike." Cam's words were few.

"Checking in on Skylar, about to leave." Cam said. He didn't introduce me, only guided me out of the room, turning to tell Skylar that we would return in the near future.

We still didn't speak to one another as we left the hospital. I waited until the hotel was once again visible to talk.

"What was all that?" I asked.

"Marry, your imagination sometimes runs wild, especially when it comes to other women, Sharon in particular. I wanted you to see what her life is really like, that she is no threat. She has enough problems without trying to make your life hell. I'll admit she seeks attention but nothing more than that."

I gasped. "Skylar is her son?" I couldn't believe what I was hearing.

"Yes, Skylar is Sharon and Ken's son. He's also one of the reasons we devote so much time and money to children and the research that will benefit them and their health even though Skylar's story is much different than the others."

I was unsure what he meant by that.

"How so?" I asked.

"Skylar is actually a product of vampire-on-vampire conception. It's not something that's supposed to happen, ever!" He emphasized.

"Any pregnancy that occurs as the result of vampire's mating always ends in self-termination. The female's body rejects the fetus under all circumstances. This is the only known case of a baby carried to term and delivered safely. There's something else you should know."

My stomach filled with butterflies, nervous about what he was going to say next.

"Sharon is not actually Wesley's daughter but because of this rare situation, she was honorarily deemed so."

I sighed, relieved.

"This protects Sharon, Skylar, and Ken on a different level, almost as royalty. After all this is vampire history in the making. Mike, he's Skylar's bodyguard. He is the best, the strongest vampire out there."

That would explain why Cam didn't have much to say to Mike. I know him well enough to understand he doesn't care for anyone who could possibly match his strength.

"All I'm trying to tell you is that woman has a lot on her mind. She has a child that she cannot bring home. A child that is severely damaged, physically. Thank goodness, his mind is in an excellent state. His I.Q. is higher than most human adults. I just want you to understand that maybe she called you Millie because for that moment, she remembered that as being your name."

I didn't approve of this lecture he was giving me. I wasn't a child. I can have my own feelings.

"So, you're......" He stopped me before I could finish

my sentence.

"Marry, I love you! I married you! If I was laughing and talking to Sharon maybe it was because I felt sorry for her. Maybe it's because I do have some compassion, regardless of what you may think. Do I want to see Sharon outside of meetings and work? Absolutely not! I cannot stress that enough! I want to spend all - every bit of my free time with you, my lovely wife and I want you to be part of every business venture that I take off on."

I sat there frozen in time, listening to his every word knowing that he does love me and only me. My heart began to soften but I doubted that I would ever rid my mind of resentment towards other women, especially the vampire ones.

"Don't start our marriage off like this, Marry. Please!" He put his hands around my waist and tugged at me until I gave in, allowing myself to fall forward, laying my head against his chest.

"Since you said please." I looked up at him and whispered.

He picked me up for the world to see and maybe they could have if it weren't the wee hours of the morning. Our coats feathered out as we flew through the night's air, landing safely on top of the hotel's roof. I could picture our silhouettes against the moon and starry sky. My hair hung over him like a cape as he protected my face from the wind. I was in awe of the city and its magnificence from our perch.

He leaned in and pressed his cold lips against mine. I felt my knees get weak as I embraced his desire. That night, high above Memphis, he proved to me that we could never be broken.

CHAPTER 2

Cam and I pulled into the driveway of our Charlotte home. The house was immensely dark from the outside, leaving me to believe none of the neighborhood had power. I was a little hesitant to get out of the car even though I knew Cam would never let anything happen to me.

Juan came around and opened my door. Cam escorted me up the steps and onto the porch, making sure I wouldn't fall. Cam put the key into the lock and turned the knob slowly. The lights immediately came on and the silence was broken.

"Surprise!" The room was filled with balloons, confetti and every friend or family member that I cared to see. Champagne bottles littered the counter, and each vampire held a dark chalice, where its contents could not be seen.

The humans gripped glasses. Both groups broke out singing happy birthday to me. The noise was beautiful, the way they harmonized was unbelievable to say the least.

As they continued singing, I kept my focus on Cam, smiling and blushing at such an event in my honor. I patted him on the chest. "I didn't want anyone to make a fuss about my birthday."

He looked down at me. "You didn't actually believe I would let this day go by without celebrating you?" He leaned over and gently kissed my forehead. "Twenty-one years old."

I could no longer hear him over the racket, but I could read his lips.

When the song was finished, Wesley chimed in with a drawn out, "And mannnnny more!" to which all in attendance shouted "Amen!" Laughter filled the space.

I thanked each one of them for showing up on my special day.

Benji had a tight hold on Sarah's hand when the two approached me, handing me a sparkly pink gift bag and wishing me the happiest of birthdays. My mouth dropped to the floor, realizing their growth. "How did this happen?" I questioned as both giggled in each other's direction.

"Come with me." I took Sarah gently by the wrist and pulled them over into a corner. The music was playing so loudly, I was sure no one could hear us. Cam and Rayan were both out on the dance floor grooving to Sam Cooke. I had become overly aware that those Rosenthal boys loved the artist and his soulful tunes.

"Well." I stared. "How did this happen?" Though I was sure Wesley played a part in this, I still needed to verify.

They were exceedingly happy to respond, both speaking at the same time. "You go ahead." Benji politely allowed Sarah to answer.

"The doctors that daddy has on staff, the ones that were originally assigned to Benji and his transition were able to extract DNA from daddy to allow us both to meet the statistics of nineteen-year-olds."

Her answer was so overwhelming that I could feel the heat from the lights beating down on my face. Not only had their physical appearance changed but mentally, they were more mature.

"As long as you both are happy, who am I to judge?" I laughed. It was odd but most everything in my life could be considered as such.

"Open your gift, Marry!" Benji insisted. I took a small box from the bag and opened it.

"Ah, these are beautiful. You didn't have to do this." I was mesmerized by the glistening ruby earrings.

"These earrings symbolize our love for you, Marry, both mine and Benji's. It also makes me think of the Wizard of Oz, where Dorothy clicked her heals together." Sarah's voice neared a whisper.

"There's no place like home." Sarah said.

"Home is wherever your family is, Marry, this is home." Benji replied.

I agreed as the three of us embraced.

They left me to dance once a slow song began to play. I recognized their closeness, Sarah and Benji were in love.

"May I have this dance, Mrs. Rosenthal?" Cam startled me from behind, requesting my presence on the dance floor with him. I could never turn him down. We had barely made two turns when Kyle and Juan alerted the party goers to a security breech out by the pool and the concern that something had been thrown into the water. Cam immediately sent me, grandmother, Sarah and Benji up to our suite for safety, locking us in behind hidden metal barriers.

We had the best security money could buy, the equivalent of an immortal F.B.I.

The four of us patiently waited for the all clear.

I found the shoe on the other foot as I comforted grandmother and her worry for Rayan. I knew in my heart that he and Cam were fine.

It felt as though hours had passed before we were set free from our guard. I was more upset that I didn't get to thank my guests than anything.

Wesley, the kids, Rayan, and grandmother stayed with us for the night.

I went up to bed and waited for Cam, he didn't show up as he normally did. I crept down the steps, following the faint distant voices, unable to make out the conversation, my curiousness grew.

My bare feet slid across the floor when I came to an abrupt halt at the dining room entrance.
Wesley, Cam, and Rayan were speaking about someone they referred to as VAM.

There had been an intruder early in the evening and a hog's head had been thrown into our swimming pool, the water was now blood red. I couldn't make out much more so in fear of being spotted I tiptoed back up to our quarters.

I wondered if it was Maggie's brother, Jon again. It

wasn't the first-time uninvited people entered our property.

When I heard Cam making his way up the steps, I quickly grabbed a book from the shelf, slid over onto the sofa and pretended to read.

His normally pale face was crimson, I assumed from anger but aware it wasn't from blood rushing to his head. He always held compassion for me during turmoil, but I was very familiar with the wrath he could unleash upon someone who held no meaning in his life.

"Cam, who is VAM?" I couldn't contain my question.

"Eavesdropping again, little girl?" He laughed as he nudged me over to the side and sat down next to me. He put his arm around me and ran his long fingernail down the front of my neck.

"Vampires Against Mortals - Do you recall the conversation where I spoke of another vampire group, strong and powerful like the EVG's?" He said.

I looked blankly into his eyes, unable to recollect that talk.

"We are deemed as equals in the eyes of some though I shall never accept such a title. Their animosity has thickened towards our group, they are now overcome with jealousy and hatred because of the unique human to vampire relationships we are capable of having. This has not been a secret, I'm not sure as to why they choose to get in a tizzy now."

I laughed at his choice of words.

"It's no joking matter. The two groups must live in peace or things will change drastically." His fangs appeared as his eyes changed to match the moonlit sky.

"I need this." He growled. "Your human blood."

I felt lightheaded and unworthy of love every time he referred to the flow that kept me alive as such. The shrieks and groans that would exit his being as he drank of me caused a subtle fright that I couldn't explain, one that left me weak but not terribly scared.

He ran his hands down my leg and then back up, allowing them to raise my gown. He pierced my inner thigh and gruesomely partook, emerging with blood dripping from his mouth down to his chin and all over his clothing. He released and ear piercing shrill that filled the room, and presumably the entire house. I worried he had taken too much.

Moments later the same awkward scream came from downstairs, I knew this time the noise came from Rayan. I didn't speak a word, aware that Cam's state of mind was still quite unsteady.

He lifted me back off the couch and moved me to the bed, where he held me tight throughout the entire night. I wondered when morning came, would we all act like none of this happened, the two vampires and their horrific release of sound.

As the sun began to shine slightly through the curtains, I woke him. "Cam?" I said.

"Yes, my dear." He responded as sweetly as ever. He didn't stop there. He pulled me in closer to him if that were at all possible. He opened his mouth extremely wide and pointed.

"Do you see that piece of metal on the back of my front tooth?" He said.

I stood on my tippy toes trying to spot what he was pointing at and there it was. "Yes, I do see it. What is it?" I asked.

"There was another device just like that one on the other side, but it's gone now." He gave me a quirky grin. "I injected it in you." He laughed.

"What?" Shocked by the thought I wanted to hit him but instead just balled my fists as a show of rage. "What is it? Why would you do that?" I asked. A million questions ran through my mind.

"Calm down!" He took my hands into his.

"At some point, in what we like to call vampire history.

it became custom that each vampire get these tracking devices – a set."

"Tracking devices, Cam?" I was outraged.

"Yes, they are used for more in-depth tracing should a vampire or close acquaintance go missing. Though we currently can locate our people supernaturally, as time goes on more technology allows for more crucial situations. A smart vampire group is always prepared." He spoke without emotion.

"Okay, but how? Are these things a danger to my body?" I needed to know. "What if I'm allergic?" I scratched my arm believing I was possibly itching at that very moment.

"Marry, stop with the dramatics already. Our group has never been as close to battle as I feel we are now, and I need to know that you are safe at every moment. If something should happen where I become unable to know your location, signals will be transferred, causing an unusual pattern to form in my brain. The waves will produce a memory like picture but in real time giving way to all the information I would need to find you."

I looked towards the floor in disbelief.

"Look at me." He placed his forefinger underneath my chin and tilted my head back up so that I was once again facing him. He placed his mouth over mine and kissed me, inserting his tongue and then quickly pulling away causing a thick string of slobber to follow.

"That was nasty." I wiped my lips with my sleeve.

He laughed like a schoolboy.

"Where is your humor, my dear?"

I couldn't find the funny in any of this.

"The tongue is very powerful. I used it to unloose the tracker from my tooth and then to press the device inside of you last night while I feasted on you." He smiled.

He pulled me in close to him. "Marry, I promise never to hurt you. Anything and everything I do is for our betterment. I hope you don't think that I found pleasure in all of this, it was actually quite a painful process. The nerves connected to each involved area of our mouths sent a horrendous amount of pressure into the gap where the metal plate once was. The shriek you heard from both Rayan and me, we could not help.

We then had to close the hole in our mouths by inserting a fang to fill the emptiness, allowing a permanent seal to form." He waited for me to respond.

"How did your fang cover the gap?" Maybe I was feeling a little bad about my reaction, but I had questions before apologizing.

"There is a small area of the fang that allows for an enamel secretion in times such as these." He explained though I didn't fully understand, the vampire anatomy was more complex than that of a human.

I was now puzzled as to why he thought a battle would ensue out of nowhere. I wasn't aware of any problems. One bloody pig head and everything was going downhill, that didn't seem logical to me. Things aren't always what they seem. I thought about Maggie's brother Jon and how he possibly had the motive to attack us. Maybe he was plotting on a deeper level than anyone could imagine. Cam, Rayan, and Wesley needed a reminder of this. I knew I couldn't be the one to tell them, though.

With Cam's convincing, I had begun to participate in more business meetings, charities, and such with him.

I've met a few of the other wives at the Children's hospital fundraisers. Women talk, no matter what species they are. VAM supposedly stands for Vampires Against Mortals but from what I hear, VAM doesn't mean anything at all. Many of the ranked VAM are even married to humans.

Rumor has it, a group of young vampires made up the horrific story after a confrontation with some mortal acquaintances, to scare them but what they have done is create a catastrophic possibility of battle. VAM was literally just VAMPIRE shortened.

    I looked over at Cam, seeing the immortal I fell in love with, the man I would do anything for. I decided to tell him how I felt once we were alone. I hoped Cam wouldn't be offended by my input. I guess if he was, it wouldn't be the first time or the last. After all, we were in this thing together and forever.

CHAPTER 3

We all said our goodbyes and then Cam and I watched our family pull out of the driveway taking two different paths. Rayan and grandmother headed back to Rhode Island as Wesley and the kids, Benji and Sarah, who were technically no longer children, travelled back to Loveland, a magical place, I suppose.

Benji and Sarah were living a real-life romance and in the most superior of places.

Cam and I held hands as we walked back into the house. I pulled him in the direction of the steps that led up to our room. He eagerly followed. I'm not sure exactly what he thought was about to transpire, but he set himself up for disappointment - or then again, maybe not, that is if he takes what I have to say well.

"Can I really talk to you about anything?" I turned to face him and then stepped backwards with each movement he made towards me.

"What's this about, Marry?" He tried to grab me as I playfully jumped out of his reach.

"Sometimes, I am bothered by the things you say and do, and I believe that's because we're different. I have no doubt that you feel the same way about my actions and opinions. That's life so it's best that you let whatever it is you are thinking - out. Holding it in would be worse for our relationship than not. Marry, I know you well enough to know if you have thought it, you are going to say it at some point. I'm listening." His attentiveness was almost frightening.

"I know you are bothered about whatever happened here last night and rightfully so. I have thought about the facts that you have, and I'm concerned that things may have been blown out of proportion." I said.

He kept listening but his breathing became heavy, nearing a growl. I remained steadfast in my statement.

"You have a hog head, one stranger, and Wesley telling you to be on guard, to protect us. That's really nothing more than before." I reached out to touch his hand, he allowed the contact which was a soothing sign.

"Babe, you know VAM, and you know that vampires cannot control their emotions. Throwing a bloody pig head into a swimming pool would be an insult to a vampire. Have you ever truly felt like VAM wanted war or to send the EVG flying into second place and take control of the world's vampire population?" I asked.

His facial expression turned grim. "No." He gave me a one-word answer.

"I'm very sorry for the things I am saying but Wesley has given a lot of himself lately – in more ways than one. You see the growth in Benji and Sarah, it's phenomenal and that's all Wesley's doing." I said.

Cam spoke up. "Skylar - Doctors have recently taken small bits of Wesley's brain tissue to insert into Skylar's frontal lobe, to help with movement. The goal is that this will help Skylar become mobile."

I gasped thinking how hard all this must be on Wesley's body. I didn't have to express my thoughts, Cam did that for me.

"There's a possibility Wesley may not be thinking as clearly as he normally would." I said.

He stood up, walked back and forth from the window a couple of times and then sat down next to me, this time closer, more intimately.

"This could result in unnecessary vampire deaths on both sides." He said, bowing his head at the thought.

"This is why EVG will always remain number one, your thoughts are in depth and realistic." I said.

He quickly took hold of my hair, jerking my head back. "Are you insulting my intelligence?" He swallowed hard. His neck pulsated from anger.

"No! Never!" I yelled. "I don't ever want you to be put

in a place where you must fight for your life. Cam, I love you and I cannot be without you!" A tear ran down my face.

His stare was cold, as blood formed in the ducts of his eyes. "I cannot exist without you, and I hope that you will take that into consideration. You are my lifeline, Marry." He stared back across the room.

The fact that he made me feel as though I was his reason for living, prompted me to allow him to feed from me once again. His touch now tender, his kisses soft, I fell asleep in his arms.

It was late in the evening before we awoke.

"In the morning, we leave for Rhode Island." He suggested that we have Juan take us. It would be like old times. We could talk, laugh, cuddle, and take in the beautiful scenery. I was excited for our journey. I felt in my heart that we were going to Rhode Island so he could be face to face with Rayan and discuss the matters at hand.

CHAPTER 4

This trip was no less exciting the hundredth time than it was the first. I may not have meant much to others, but I believed I was everything to my Cam. I laughed at the thought, remembering how grandmother and mother used to call him, my Cam, when I was younger. I never believed it at the time.

The road underneath the car made a slight rumble as we pulled out onto the main road.

"What exactly are you going to say to Rayan?" I continued to look out the window.

Cam began to roll up the petition between us and Juan "You don't mind do you, brother? I need to talk to my wife for a little while." Cam mischievously grinned when Juan glanced back at us.

"No sir, Cam." Juan replied in a hurry and as quick as that, we were separated from our driver.

"I have a lot to say to him, Marry. Rayan is a very smart man and I'm quite sure he has already thought about the things you and I discussed. All the procedures and DNA swaps are sure to have caused some damage to Wesley. We will discuss having him seen by a new physician, someone other than the crafty doctor who has helped with the surgical removals and placements. He needs a new start; I suppose you could say." He placed his cold hand upon my leg, chilling me just enough that I shook.

"I'm sorry." He whispered.

"No, it's not you! It's me! All this excitement has me a little on edge." I'm not sure if he believed me or not, I was just thankful my actions didn't stir up a fuss.

"Wesley is so much more than a leader to us, Marry. He's like a father. In our eyes his strength is beyond measure and to think his mind has possibly been affected by his good deeds is very disheartening."

I understood exactly what he was saying.

"I will be releasing Wesley's Doctor Do Good from all his duties upon our arrival." He looked towards the ceiling to prevent the laughter that was brewing; doctor do good.

I smirked, rather tickled at his humor.

"I believe him to have become obsessed with the fortune he is making, no longer setting standards for Wesley's care. I have someone else in mind to oversee him medically, a gentleman I met in Memphis a year or so ago. His knowledge is extensive, I have been following his work and am intrigued." Cam said.

I had no idea he was already considering changing Wesley's doctor. I felt much better knowing that I was clearly not the first to question the medical advice Wesley was receiving.

"His name is Dr. Patak, he's from Mandalay, a city in Myanmar. I shall take you there one day."

The vampire life was luxurious.

"He's already working on a new project for me." He chuckled.

"Really? What?" I asked.

"You will know when the time is right." He raised his eyebrows and blinked a few times. I moved towards him to give him a peck on the cheek. He was the most handsome creature I had ever laid eyes on and that would never change.

The smile on his face was no longer visible. "We've got to get Wesley checked out and fast." He said.

The problem was going to be convincing Wesley that something was wrong with him. He was strong-willed and had always overseen everything and everyone, with the tables now turning, Cam feared a rebuttal.

It felt good to spot grandmother's house once we made it up the steep hill, this was truly home for me even after all the horrific events that had taken place here.

Juan hurried and opened the car door for Cam and me then carried our bags in and directly to our rooms.

Cam walked up to Rayan, the two shook hands. Rayan pulled Cam in close. "Brother." He spoke using their term of endearment.

"Who's staying in the bunker out back?" Cam asked Rayan, raising my suspicion that they could possibly smell each other, I laughed at the thought. I mean, how else would he know there was a visitor.

A disappointed Rayan told him that Read was in the bunker. He knew that wouldn't sit well with Cam.

"He didn't have anywhere else to go. Well, he had places to go but he preyed on my kindness and practically begged me to stay here, let us not forget, the bunkers can be used by any of our vampires." Rayan said.

Cam just shook his head.

"He's in a state of depression. All he does is sit down there and read those books. Come on now little brother - our mother loved him for some reason and went as far as to wed him. We can't just do him badly." Rayan said having always been the nicer of the two brothers. The truth is the truth.

"Come on in and get settled." Rayan waved us down the corridor.

I was tired from the trip, dragging my feet. Cam, not so much. He flashed me a gentle smile and then joined Rayan as he headed back to the study.

Grandmother met me in the hallway, patted me on my back and escorted me up to my old room where Cam and I always stayed when we visited Rhode Island. She took my hand in hers; I could feel her hand lotion seeping its oiliness onto me.

"Good night, dear." She strolled a few steps and then disappeared into her room without her beloved Rayan.

I was immediately reminded of the creepy incident back at home, imagining Rayan injecting my grandmother's thigh with a tracking chip made me a tad bit ill. The quicker I went to sleep, the better - or so I thought.

I was awakened by a loud hissing and the sound of furniture being thrown around downstairs.

Grandmother, in her robe, snuck around the corner and into my room. "Dear Lord, Marry, those boys somehow convinced Wesley to come here last night - alone. He brought none of his staff, not a single one! Whatever they've said to him has him in some kind of super-natural uproar." She was nervous and shaking.

"Grandmother, I have got to go check on Cam!" I screamed.

"Do not to go down there. As your grandmother, I forbid you. He is a grown man!" Her attempt at stern assertiveness didn't work. I threw on some clothes and began to tip toe quietly down the steps.

Grandmother let out a deep sigh and stayed there in my room.

The noises were getting louder. I could hear glass shattering as I slyly approached the Study door. I peeked around to see Wesley's face cold; he froze his movements and focused hard on the rooms void. I knew exactly what this meant, he had summoned other vampires. This situation was beyond terrible for the EVG's leader to call for help. There was nothing I could do. I ran to the dining room and hid under the table. I was now fearful for my own safety. We were all about to die!

A gust of wind sent my hair flying, my vision blurred, it had to be a vampire swooshing past me. I was concerned which member may have answered Wesley's call.

"Read!" I heard Rayan from the other room. I got out from under the table and softly walked back to the Study. Thank goodness, Read was the one closest to the situation. I looked in again, this time to see Wesley pinned high in the corner of the ceiling, his arms stretched out and his gruesome, grimy nails dug into the wall. He hovered there, hissing. He knocked the bookshelf over, glass shelving shattered all over the floor.

Wesley's fangs were longer and more pronounced than Cam's. His skin color was a mix of Rayan's yellow and Cam's gray. He was a tainted green, dirty looking. His eyes didn't glow, they were red, bleeding from the inside as if pressure had built up within them, his morbid tears unable to release.

He forcefully pushed his body forward from the wall with such strength that it caused Cam, Rayan, and Read to back away. The three of them, fully changed, were playing defense to Wesley's offense. They didn't want to hurt him, only subdue him but they also didn't want to be injured in the process.

They hissed back, waving their arms back and forth at him. Read quickly backed out of the room, almost tripping over me because of my position. He stopped and looked at me, fear filled my soul. But, just as fast as he moved out of the room – He changed back into his human form.

"Marry, go get a candle and matches, hurry!" I sped off as he opened the black duffle bag he carried with him, retrieving a syringe.

Grandmother once again met me, having heard his request, she handed off his needs.

Read set fire to the candle but he didn't freeze as others would have.

He changed back into vampire and entered once again into the Study. Cam and Rayan came out immediately.

The screeching and hissing between Wesley and Read deafened me. I couldn't help but think Read was on a suicide mission. Then like after a storm - there was calm. A silence that was more frightening to me than all the commotion.

Rayan and Cam were back to human. Cam held me close. Rayan did the same to my grandmother.

"He's quite ill." Cam whispered in my ear.

The experience was traumatic for us all. We waited patiently in the foyer to see who would emerge. Cam and

Rayan both stood motionless, worried about both men.

Read swiftly came to our side, everyone breathed a sigh of relief.

"We must move fast, fellas. I injected him with a serum that will keep him immobile for a short time." Read said.

A local nurse with ties to the family showed up immediately and had Wesley moved to Memphis by flight.

The cause of this whole outburst was Cam and Rayan's attempt to get him to go willingly. I knew for a fact had the shoe been on the other foot, Cam and Rayan would've also refused.

Once Wesley was well enough, he would realize this was done out of love.

"We're all going to Memphis with Wesley." Rayan instructed the group.

"This is what a real family does, sticks together, especially during difficult times." Rayan said.

Cam notified Benji and Sarah of the situation. They would catch the first flight to Tennessee.

It seemed odd that we were traveling to Memphis to have Wesley examined by a doctor at the Children's Hospital but the EVG's had put a lot of time and resources into the facility. The doctors there were better equipped than any to handle a vampire emergency. They had familiarized themselves with the vampire make-up, from top to bottom. These are the exact doctors that were trusted with treating and caring for Skylar.

Sometimes I find myself believing and feeling as if I am vampire, my whole life revolves around immortals. Everything that I love except for my grandmother is considered death maintaining on earth. I feel dark at times, I'm not the same full of life little girl that I once was. I'm happy but I'm still adjusting.

We all sat patiently and in silence on the trip to Memphis, Cam encouraged us not to worry as Dr. Patak, Cam's new hire physician, was awaiting Wesley's arrival.

"Everything will be fine." He winked at me, still able to give me butterflies.

I prayed that he was right.

CHAPTER 5

It was dark when the plane touched down. Cam alerted us that Benji and Sarah would be landing in a matter of minutes. The pilot let down the steps. Rayan helped grandmother down first.

"Good Lord." Her first words upon exit. "This Tennessee heat is in full effect."

That was nothing abnormal for the state. The humidity ruined my hair, the curls fell out immediately, and frizz took over. I was sure the few beads of sweat I felt rolling down my forehead destroyed my makeup.

I watched as Wesley was rushed into the hospital through a delivery door in the back near the dock normally used for supplies. Rayan led the way in, we all followed close behind.

The only thing you could hear besides silence was the sound of the gurney rolling quickly across the hospital floor. Oh, and the noise our heals made as Sarah and I trotted along, arm in arm with the men who spoiled us beyond belief. There was no confusion as to why the group was called Elite. You would've known that from the homes we lived in, the cars we drove, and our attire, A-1, always dressed to the tee.

Since marriage, I strived to be high class whenever we were outside of our home. It came with the territory, I suppose. I represent Cam and he represents The EVG's.

Wesley was still sedated - Thank goodness! I can just imagine the horrific scene if he were coherent.

The doctor raised his hand to stop our movements. Cam was displeased with this, he hissed under his breath, I hoped I was the only one that could hear him. We were directed into a waiting room. The doctor calmed the situation by sending a member of his team in to speak with Cam and Rayan telling them that Wesley was going to receive the best care possible.

"Follow me, gentlemen." He escorted Cam and Rayan through a door marked *Do Not Enter*. Cam turned back to me and nodded, letting me know everything was okay.

Read left, stating he was going back to the property, fearful of how Wesley may respond when he wakes up.

Once they were out of sight, the rest of us were taken into an adjacent room, red leather couches outlined the black walls. Dimmed lights lit up as much of the space as possible. A crème-colored rug covered at least two thirds of the floor. I couldn't keep my eyes off of it.

"It's an antique Persian rug, dear." Grandmother leaned over and whispered. "Gorgeous, isn't it? Have Cam purchase you one upon your return home." I took note.

"Vending machines? Really?" Benji hurried over to them, calling out every snack and soft drink they held. "A little discriminatory, don't you think?" He laughed and then offered me an apology. "I sometimes forget you're human." He laughed.

"As do I." I responded, now standing in front of the contraption, contemplating purchasing a goodie. Sarah giggled at us both as grandmother lowered her head.

The room was now eerily quiet, I chose not to buy anything mostly because I was bothered by not being able to see Sarah and Benji's reflection in the glass, rarely did I notice such but today it was quite evident. I lost my appetite.

Benji and Sarah curled up in the corner, holding hands and cuddling. Grandmother sat alone with her legs crossed, rummaging through her purse.

I jumped ten feet in the air startled by Cam and Rayan's reappearance. Cam's face had become unfamiliar; his color was abnormal. "Cam." I shouted.

Rayan quickly went to his side. "Brother, come with me, you too, Marry." He demanded.

We all three went into an empty office, directly across from the waiting room. Rayan helped Cam over to a chair and then gently shut the door trying to avoid unnecessary attention.

"Brother, when's the last time you fed?" He asked.

"I've missed my last two appointments. It's no big deal, I'm fine." Cam struggled to get his words out. I was outraged by his lack of self-care.

"I've had a lot going on, in the midst of a project." Cam said.

I was hurt knowing that he let himself get in this state.

"Cam, you know your meals could've been delivered directly to your home. This just doesn't make any sense to me, brother." Rayan was very concerned.

"My work is my priority as of now." Cam said. What vampire does not put blood first, his thought was ludicrous. He was speaking out of his mind.

Rayan turned towards me and placed his clammy hand on my knee. I knew what was coming next. I was no stranger to this.

"Yes, I'll feed him." I said, before he could even ask the question.

Cam jumped up with furry in his already discolored eyes, forbidding me to let him drink of my blood. I froze, dumbfounded at his rebuke.

"What is going on here?" Rayan asked. One of Rayan's fangs exposed itself. He covered his mouth with his fingers.

"She can't, Marry needs all of her strength, giving me her blood could damage my plans for her." Cams seriousness frightened me.

"Your plans for me?" I asked.

Rayan tried to laugh off the situation.

"Marry, could you please excuse us for just a moment?" Rayan said. His teeth now back in their place, he opened the door for me like the gentleman he always was.

When he summoned me back in the room, Cam fed off me but just enough to regain his normal color and some strength. Rayan assured me that this type of thing happens every now and again.

"He'll be fine. His malnutrition caused him to speak slightly out of the head earlier, but I've determined no cause to worry." Rayan said, then he informed me a member of the EVG food bank would be here shortly to make sure he was caught up on all his nutrients. I have always appreciated Rayan's ability to calm me down with words.

The three of us rejoined the family in the waiting area.

"Clear" I thought my ears deceived me. Then again "Clear." The doctor's voice echoed through the area.

"Has his heart stopped? What are they doing to him?" I cried out in desperation, fearful for Wesley's life. This sparked laughter from everyone around. "There is nothing funny here!" I felt my face heat with anger.

Cam gracefully put his arms around me "Marry, my dear. Wesley is a vampire. He did not code."

I brought my hands up and covered my eyes in embarrassment. Cam guided me to the sofa and the two of us sat down. Just as we had begun to take the lover's quiz in a popular magazine, the doctor reappeared.

"Mr. Rosenthal, may I speak with you and your brother once more, please?" He asked. The three headed out back across the hall only to be stopped by a frantic Sharon pulling her husband Ken through the corridor.

"Where is my daddy? Is he okay?" She headed straight for Cam. Not today, sister! I quickly moved out into the hall and placed myself in between Sharon and Cam. He pulled me in closer to clarify he would no longer console her, no matter her troubles. She had Ken for that.

She swung her head, her hair went flying, nearly smacked us both in the face. She then flung herself into Ken's arms. Ken dabbed at her fake tears with the purple handkerchief he had placed in his suite pocket and assured her everything would be fine.

Turns out, everything was going to be fine. Rayan called

us together as a group and hushed those of us who could not control our emotions, Sharon.

"It appears that Wesley had an adverse reaction because of the amount of DNA that he has allowed to be taken from him and used to help Skylar and so many others. These procedures have taken a toll on his mind and caused quite a bit of memory loss. The doctor has advised that he should remain here, in this hospital, for at least another seventy-two hours, in which time he should be as good as new. Normally, our genetic make-up would have allowed our bodies to heal and replenish all matter taken from us but because it was so much, so fast, Wesley's body was unable to keep up. We will be able to see him in the morning." We waited for Rayan to complete his update before we all cheered with excitement. "Some of us will be staying at The Peabody should any of you want to join." He added.

I was personally thrilled about staying at The Peabody! They have live ducks in their lobby. I mean, who in their right mind doesn't want to see a duck march?

Cam had his dinner and then he and Rayan went to visit with Wesley for a while longer. He was doing well but still very tired just as the doctor explained.

I believed it was Wesley's sickness that caused his delusions about VAM. I hoped Cam and Rayan agreed and that any sort of altercation with the group could be avoided.

"Sarah, your father wishes to see you." Rayan solemnly escorted her to the room from whence he and Cam emerged. The rest of us would see him tomorrow but he couldn't go any length of time without seeing his baby girl.

She was only in there for about ten minutes before returning, she wiped her tear-stained eyes. I knew the pain of watching a parent in such a state. I walked towards her to try and comfort her, but Benji sped past me and quickly embraced her. Cam looked at me and laughed.

I threw my hands up. "Oh, to be young again and newly in love." I said.

Cam's laughter quickly ceased. "Every morning when we wake up, our love is fresh and exciting." He said taking me by the hand and nearly pulling me to the car. He didn't give Juan a chance to open the door, he did it himself. He made Juan start the engine, immediately rolling up the partition between us and Juan. He ripped off his own shirt, placing my hands upon his muscular chest, he kissed me with such passion and a force so strong that I believed I passed out having no recollection of what happened next.

CHAPTER 6

Juan stopped the car directly under the canopy at the entrance to the Peabody. Cam and I got out. I held my head down wondering if I allowed myself to make mortifying noises on the journey here, still puzzled as to why I lost some of my memory.

Cam's energy had skyrocketed, possibly from the double dose of sustenance. I wasn't the least bit tired, either. Even after such a long wait at the Children's Hospital and whatever else went on during the car ride here.

The Hotel gleamed magnificently, plants and trees scattered throughout the lobby. The lighting was perfect for any mood, brightly shining through the darkness of a makeshift city forest and in the center of it all, a pond for the precious duckies. My biggest thrill, however, came from reading the sign that pointed to an indoor swimming pool.

Cam reserved the Romeo and Juliet suite for us. The room was more like an apartment with a loft. A spiral staircase ascended to the inner get-a-way from a two-story parlor with a rather unnecessary fireplace that took me by surprise. It was beautiful to look at. I remembered seeing this place in an issue of the Better Homes and Gardens magazine when I was younger. The article was amazing. It reflected on guests, presidents - new and old, celebrities and even a ghost that supposedly haunts the eleventh floor. The thrill of the supernatural made me want to stay here for at least a week so I didn't miss out on anything. Chills ran through me, making the tiny hairs on my arms stand up when I realized we were staying on the eleventh floor. I didn't tell Cam the ghost story and I doubted very seriously he would be frightened by a ghost.

I went into the bedroom, rummaged through my luggage, and pulled out the red bikini I brought along in case an opportunity like this one should arise. I slipped it on and paraded around Cam until he finally looked up from some paperwork, he seemed to be studying awfully hard. He smiled, grabbed me, and then pulled me down onto his lap. He gave me a peck on the cheek.

"The hint of this bathing suit could be construed in many different ways, my dear. What is it that you want?" He grinned.

"Oh, Cam you know how much I love the pool. Let's go swimming, neither one of us is tired and it would be a great way to unwind and spend some quality time together. The pool is indoors and secluded in the basement. I just think it would be exciting."

He agreed and changed into his long swimming trunks and a white T-shirt. He never showed all his body, not in public. I'm not sure why that was, his muscular physique was a treat for any set of eyes. On second thought, I didn't want anyone else gawking at his beauty. He's my perfect Cam, for always.

"The pink or blue one?" He held up two terry cloth towels.

"I choose pink."

"Excellent, because I choose blue." I almost felt like we were talking about something else, maybe the gender of future off springs.

We walked hand in hand down to the elevator, the door slowly opened and creaked as we stepped on.

"Maybe we should have taken the stairs." I said, uneasy from the sound it made.

"If this thing malfunctions, I promise to hover here with you in my arms until help arrives." Cam laughed as he pressed the button leading to our destination. He moved his head back and forth to the horrible music. "What?" He laughed again. The doors opened and he darted out.

"Race ya! Never mind, that would be unfair." Cam joked. He scooped me up and carried me to the pool, we both went crashing into the deep end. I screamed and kicked, splashing water all over him. We had the pool to ourselves.

Intertwined in each other's arms we bobbed up and down in the same spot, sharing a sweet kiss. I gasped, regaining my breath.

I felt as though we were being watched. It wouldn't be the first time and undoubtedly not the last. I prayed it wasn't the Peabody ghost on a mission. Surely this place wasn't really haunted.

I was pleased that Sharon and Ken chose not to stay and flew back to Wesley's estate in Loveland though it didn't make sense to me how they could leave their son in that hospital and not be with him all the time. He had been there since birth. The thought infuriated me.

"What's wrong, Marry?" Cam lifted me up slightly and then brought me back down so that we were once again eye level with each other. The lights shimmered off the water's small ripple allowing for a twinkle to form in Cam's beautiful eyes.

He guided me to shallow end, pulling himself up by the metal railing, and coaxing me out of the pool with promises of something more pleasurable. He sat down on a folding chair, leaned over and rubbed his legs dry with the blue towel. I continued to stand, admiring my husband and the strength he carried no matter where we were. The glow in his eyes remained as he looked up at me.

"I want you to have my child." He spoke quietly as he looked into my eyes with such adoration. I was at a loss for words.

"I don't want to wait. There's nothing I want more than to be a father, Marry. I hope you agree." He said.

"Cam." I could only say his name.

"Dr. Patak has mastered the science, we can become parents if we choose to." He said. I immediately jumped back into the pool, cupping my hands, and sending water flying back in his direction.

"Marry, stop! This is a serious matter!" He reprimanded me.

Out the corner of my eye, I caught a glimpse of a woman, but only her outline. I screamed, trying to run through the water to get back out of the pool. Cam reached down and lifted me to the edge of the concrete with one arm.

"What is wrong with you? Did you see a ghost or something?" Cam laughed at my hysterics.

I pulled him towards the red exit sign.

He jerked me back. "What is going on?" His tone changed, his fangs slightly visible, his breath heavy in my face. He shook me. "What is it?" He asked again.

I pointed back in the opposite direction. "A lady, a figure, she wasn't human." I buried my head in his chest and began to weep. "I don't know why you're laughing." I cried harder.

"You silly girl, you are not afraid of vampires, but a little ghost causes you tears?" He kissed me on the forehead; unbothered.

"Let's go back to the room." I pleaded with him to leave the area even though no further signs of the creepy woman existed.

"No, my dear." He pulled me back towards the chairs, my sandals catching on every groove as I tried to prohibit the return.

"This conversation needs to be had and we will have it now." He insisted with total disregard for my feelings. "As my wife are you willing to carry my baby? Are you willing to at least try? We have talked about this before sweetheart, it's no secret that I want children and with you." He stared blankly at me.

The room became a blur. I knew that he had spent millions to make his dream come true.

He was sincere and I knew I at least owed him a response.

When my dizziness subsided, and I was able to think once again, I answered him.

"I don't know too many women who don't want children but I'm unsure of what you are asking of me. What would such a procedure consist of?" I told him my fears and as always, he reassured me that nothing could go wrong. He believed highly in himself and his kind.

"Marry, you and I have an appointment to meet with Dr. Patak after we visit Wesley tomorrow, either you come with me, or I will go alone. I can tell you this with honesty, it will be unacceptable for you to deny me this and you can take that to mean whatever you wish."

I pulled away from him, crushed, feeling as though I was meaningless.

Angrily, he moved me back where he wanted me. My face heated up as insults churned within my being, words that I would never release.

"My life doesn't matter to you, Cam? Is that what you're saying? You would put me in danger for a child that we aren't sure can exist. A child that I may not be able to carry! A child that could come out to be like Skylar! Is that what you want? A Skylar?" I screamed.

He let go of my arm. I threw my towel around my cold wet body and walked furiously to the elevator, he scooped me up and carried me back to our quarters.

"We don't need this fight, Marry." I laid my head on his shoulder and closed my eyes. I didn't know how to fix this.

He bypassed the staircase and flew me directly to the loft. He protectively laid me down on the bed. "Get some rest, I love you." I found comfort hearing that he still loved me.

"Where are you going?" I asked.

"Downstairs, I'll be just a scream away." He winked.

I fell asleep for what seemed like no time. My eyes popped open, the room was dark, and Cam now lay beside me. I felt secure knowing he was in bed with me, but something was off about my surroundings. A glowing bluish haze filled the air, a bright gleam crept through the window, I presumed radiating from the streetlight. A faint squeaking noise from below made its way to my ears.

I slid quietly from under the sheets, gently placing my feet on the floor. I walked barefoot so not to be heard, over to the spiral staircase and peered down into the living area. The rocking chair was now positioned by the fireplace. It eerily rocked back and forth. I could see a woman's silhouette, her mid length hair slightly hung over the back of the chair. She was holding something, rocking calmly. She never turned to face me.

"Hello." My voice shaking, I called out.

She didn't respond. I thought about waking Cam, but my gut feeling was to let him sleep through whatever this was. "Hello." I said, a little louder this time, peacefully.

"Marry" My name exited her lips as she turned to face me.

"Momma?" I trembled in fear before realizing I was stuck in my position, unable to move or scream, I could only stand there and listen.

She stood up from the rocking chair holding a baby. I figured this all to be a dream.

"Mother, am I dreaming? Are you really here?" I asked.

She answered me as if she were still living "Marry, you would not confuse me with another, would you? I am your mother, and this Marry, is your son. She held the baby out towards me, swaddled in a light blue blanket. Marry, if you take the vows you made with Cam seriously then you will give him the child he desires. He loves you, Marry. Was there ever a time in which he did not give you whatever your heart desired, including love, my dear?"

The way she spoke to me, the things she said, made me believe it was truly my mother. I wanted to say so much more to her but just as quickly as she appeared, she was gone. A cloudy mist was left covering the chair. I needed my mother. I stood there for nearly an hour hoping for her return, no such luck.

How stupid I had been, I realized she came to me, advising me to change my heart, this was the one thing that could possibly destroy my marriage if I didn't bend.

I was left with the image of her holding my infant son. I climbed back into bed trying not to wake Cam. I could no longer sleep.

The sun began to shine through our window, I got up and pulled the curtains a little tighter. Cam yawned and sat up on the side of the bed. I didn't let him get a word out.

"Shhhh. Let me talk." I said. I walked over to his side of the bed and gently placed my finger over his mouth. He growled and pretended to bite at it. "We can meet with Dr. Patak today. This is what I want. I know the two of us together will do an awesome job of raiding a child!"

He roared as he lifted me high above his head, the joy in his laughter was contagious! I felt nearly as happy as the day we married.

"Why the sudden change of heart? I have to ask." He hugged me tightly, rocking me back and forth.

"Morning breath! Ugh!" I giggled, still kissing him with such enthusasm that he almost forgot I hadn't answered his question. None the less, I went ahead with my response as I backed slowly away from him. "I love you with everything in me. We are a team, and I will never give you anything less than my best."

His smile revealed his pearly white teeth, no fangs in sight. I admired his perfect facial features and his toned body. Many were jealous of what was mine.

"Cam, there is one thing I need." He tilted his head and frowned, confused as to what he had not provided me with.

"Your wish is my command." He spoke softly.

"I want that rocking chair from downstairs brought to our home in Charlotte, no matter the cost." I pointed towards it, still placed in front of the fireplace.

"Yes ma'am, consider it done." The conversation was over at that moment, decisions had been made.

CHAPTER 7

"Doc says only one person at a time allowed back to see Wesley." Rayan said when he met us at the entrance to the hospital. We followed him back down the corridor, he turned to face Cam as we walked. "He's doing much better." Rayan said as he winked at me.

We continued towards Wesley's room. There were chairs placed right outside of the door, three on each side nearly taking up all the hallway space. I greeted grandmother who occupied one of them by kissing her on both sides of her cheeks, she did the same in return.

"Sarah and Benjmain just left. She was here nearly before the sun went down." Rayan grinned.

"Wesley wants to see you next, Marry." I looked at Cam for approval, puzzled by the request. I would've thought Cam to be next on the list. Cam nodded and shrugged his shoulders, allowing me to proceed.

I gently tapped on the door, announcing my entrance.

"Come in." Wesley's voice was weak but clear.

It was awkward seeing Wesley like that, he wasn't attached to tubing or wires, no machines, but the sight of him in a hospital bed unnerved me. He was very much aware of what was going on and his appearance was a hundred times better. He chuckled when I came in the room, grabbed my hand and kissed it just like he always did.

"You thought I lost my mind, didn't you, Marry?" He laughed again.

I just smiled, unsure of how to respond to a question with a less than desirable true answer.

"You should be back to normal in no time if you're feeling the way you look." We both laughed, flattery had been known to win Wesley over. He had always been the biggest flirt I knew. He patted the side of the bed, insisting I sit next to him.

"Marry, there is something I need to talk to you about. I'm not sure why I've chosen you to tell this too but you're a smart girl and I value and trust your opinion."

I could feel my eyes widen.

"Do you feel comfortable with the two of us having a private and confidential conversation?" He asked. "This is something you cannot tell Cam. I need your word on this, Marry."

Now I was truly frightened, keeping a secret from my husband was not a good idea, no matter who suggested it. I feared he was still sick, unable to think properly.

"Honestly, I'm uncomfortable keeping anything from Cam." Believing in my mind if what he disclosed needed to be heard by Cam, I would go against my word.

"Understandable." He stared blankly at me, arousing my curiosity. Now, I had to hear what was on his mind.

"Out of the utmost respect for you, I will listen and offer any insight I may have, sir." I said.

The awkwardness elevated.

He began to speak in a low tone. "When I came here to this hospital to give Skylar more of my DNA, the doctors gave me some very disturbing news." I paid very close attention to what he was saying, detail was a must in our world.

"You are no stranger to the VAM group. I know that you have met a few of them at charity events, meetings, and the likes thereof." I nodded, agreeing with his statement.

"Well." He said before coughing.

I offered him a rag to which he declined.

"My grandson by adoption, Skylar, is not just part of the EVG group." He said.

I was sure he was still delusional, until he told me otherwise.

"Some of the doctors here also work with VAM and study their bloodline as well as their genealogy. It's clear that Sharon is Skylar's mother, but Ken is surely not his father. Skylar is half and half. He's mixed with VAM and EVG. This is a disgrace to our group, and it will bring just as much shame to VAM." He scoffed.

I didn't know how to respond so I kept listening.

"I could keep this a secret and go on like it hasn't happened but there are several reasons why I can't do that. First, this makes Sharon a traitor and she will have to be dealt with accordingly."

The idea of that didn't bother me much.

"Secondly, in order for my grandson to survive and one day live a normal vampire life, he is going to need a healthy DNA transplant from a VAM member." He looked down at the floor.

Maybe he was going to ask me to kill Sharon. Shame on me for thinking I could and would if the request was made known. I couldn't imagine anything as unforgivable as knowing that Skylar could've been well by now had Sharon confessed her sins. I was still curious as to why Wesley was telling me this. He answered that without me asking just like Cam does when he knows my wheels are spinning about something.

"I want you to make sure you attend every meeting that Sharon is at. Take note of which VAM she favors. You and I will meet again." I agreed, we hugged, and I left the room like nothing was ever said. I guess I would keep his secret, but I wasn't sure for how long.

Cam smiled when I came out of the room. He put his arm around me and directed me over to where the rest of the family was standing. Benji and Sarah were back to bid us all farewell. They were about to fly back to Colorado on Wesley's jet. With my newfound information, I was a little nervous about this, knowing that Sharon and Ken were already there.

Sarah had always travelled with an entourage of security personnel, but I guess with Wesley not there to direct her, she had taken it upon herself to dismiss the detail so that she and Benji could travel alone.

"Sarah, can I speak with you for a moment?" I took her by the hand and led her down the hall as far as I could, with an abrupt turn, I addressed her. "Girl talk!" Though it was much more serious than that. "Where is your staff? I asked. "Your dad never let you go anywhere without them before, why the sudden change?"

She sighed, tried to shrug me off and headed back towards the group.

"I care!" I said just above a whisper knowing that she could still hear me.

She allowed her arms to drop by her side, a clapping noise echoed when her hands bounced off her legs and then she moped back towards me.

"Look, I understand, sweetie. I know you want time alone with Benji, just the two of you. I was that girl once, Sarah. It's okay and normal to want that. I'm not fussing at you. I just want you to be safe and well protected. This world is crazy!" That was the biggest understatement of the year! "Sarah, always expect the unexpected and watch your surroundings. Keep your staff on duty. They're not going to tell Wesley anything that you don't want him to know, I can assure you of that. I'm quite sure he knows everything, anyways. Your dad is no dummy by any means."

We both knew that to be a fact.

I smiled, she smiled and then she hugged me forcefully around the neck while standing on her tiptoes. She couldn't begin to imagine her own strength. "I love you, Marry. I will do as you have asked." She said.

I sighed, relieved.

"Thank you, Sarah. I love you too, more than you could possibly know." I viewed her as a daughter.

I found myself daydreaming about the child that Cam and I would soon have. I didn't doubt Cam one bit and I knew the time was coming.

Immobile from my thoughts, grandmother took ahold of my shoulder, startling me. "Rayan and I are going back to the Peabody, Sarah and Benji have already left." Grandmother said. I wondered how long I had been standing here, alone.

The buzzing from the light fixture above reminded me of my past and gave a hint to the bright future ahead, maybe I was excited for motherhood. Butterflies overtook my stomach.

Rayan waved to grandmother trying to hurry her up. I kissed her goodbye and waited for Cam to advise me of our next move.

"Let's go check on Skylar, shall we? We have a few minutes to spare." Cam said. Hand in hand we walked towards the elevator.

I felt uncomfortable carrying with me the information of Skylar's secret VAM identity. But I needed to keep it as long as I could.

Cam released his grip on me and darted towards Skylar's door which was completely shut, out of the norm. He knocked out of courtesy with his fingers already touching the knob. When he went unanswered, his fangs became visible. "You wait here." His tone turned gruff and harsh.

I felt the anxiety pour through my body; something was off.

Cam let out an unfamiliar shrill.

Against his wishes, I slightly opened the door noticing him on his knees, his hand placed over his head, glancing over at me with a look of desperation. "Stay out!" He screamed.

I couldn't.

He was now fully vampire, his face blood stained with tears. He wept in pain from what appeared to be heartbreak. I had never seen him like this before. I walked slowly in his direction, realizing Skylar's bodyguard was in pieces, sprawled out over the room, his head lay feet from the rest of him. I moved carefully across the blood tainted floor and reached for the blue curtain that was pulled shut around Skylar's bed.

Cam screamed out once again in horror.

I flung the curtain open to find Skylar gasping for breath, trying his best to hold on to life. His neck perforated. Someone sliced right through his child skin in order to take him out of this world.

Skylar's words were stuck, he reached for me, slipping in and out of consciousness.

"Get a doctor!" I yelled at the top of my lungs.

Cam didn't move. He gazed into my eyes, his fangs pointed and ready for attack. His color had become sickening. He pointed his animal finger at me, the nail curled around from the monstrosity's length.

"You stay here. No one in or out!" He rose from his position. "I will return."

Within a matter of seconds, he, and Rayan, as vampires, stood over Skylar.

They granted entrance to a group of men, all in long white coats that zipped up the front, stopping just below the chin. A female nurse close behind, single handedly moved Skylar's body onto a new and clean gurney. He was rolled out of the room before I could bat an eye.

"Where are they taking him?" I spoke to whomever would listen. No one responded to any of my questions, not even Cam. I began to cry, my emotions uncontainable. He must've felt the tremendous hurt that overcame me or at least I thought he did.

"Brother, I'll be back." Cam in a rush, took me down to Wesley's room and left me there. "Go in, act like you're visiting. You mustn't say a word about this to Wesley." Cam's actions seemed foolish. Wesley would feel what was going on, he would know his grandson was in danger.

"What's wrong, dear?" Wesley motioned for me to

come closer. I had a visual of two small pieces of enamel making their way through his upper gum. I couldn't hold back my tears any longer. I answered him truthfully and I didn't care if Cam found out.

"We went to visit Skylar, there were some oddities as we approached the room. When we entered in, we found Mike dead on the floor. Blood was everywhere!" I spoke fast, almost in hysterics.

Wesley took a deep breath. "And Skylar?"

"Skylar is alive, but he has some damage! Someone was trying to kill him, Wesley. His throat was slit, nearly from ear to ear. He tried to speak but couldn't." I said.

A subtle hiss unleashed itself from Wesley, but he remained composed.

"Cam called for the cleanup crew to take care of Mike and then Skylar was wheeled away at Cam's demand. I don't know where they went, any of them. I don't know what's going on!" I was crying so hard by now, I bent down to get a handkerchief from my purse and by the time I looked back up, Wesley was gone!

I stomped my feet, grabbed my bag, pulled myself together and I left, too. I had class about myself, I wasn't about to be tossed to the side like a piece of garbage. This was too much! Every time a speckle of happiness appeared in our lives, something surreal had to come in and crash it. I was left in unsafe territory and nothing about that was okay with me.

I headed towards the door with my high heels and Gucci bag. I kept my head up, abruptly I made a left turn. Today, I was going out the human exit. I spoke to every single person I passed by and don't think for one moment some of those handsome doctors didn't give me the eye. I'm not old, I'm just married … to a vampire. A Vampire that would soon find himself in a where's his wife situation. He just doesn't know it yet.

I debated going back to the Peabody and getting a room

knowing that my grandmother was most likely there. I called Cherry back in Charlotte; she had always been such a help to me. She was an excellent caregiver for my mother up until her passing. I considered her a friend, a confidant. She booked me the next flight out of Memphis, nonstop to Charlotte, and it left in an hour.

I called for Juan to meet me at the front entrance of the hospital. He appeared out of nowhere.

"Mr. Rosenthal does not need to know where I'm headed or even where I am for that matter. Neither of the Rosenthal men and especially not Wesley." I fumed.

Juan agreed he would not tell them. I tipped him a hundred and all for naught, I had a tracking device in my thigh. I slumped down into the leather seat and closed my eyes.

Maybe my departure would wake Cam up to the way he has treated me, all of which is unacceptable, especially if he's going to make demands out of me, like having a child.

I boarded the plane and had Kyle, another member of our staff, retrieve me from the Charlotte International Airport. I was home in no time. Cherry fixed me supper, I ate, took a shower and got in bed. I wondered how long it would take Cam to come to me.

CHAPTER 8

I was awakened by a knock at our bedroom door. It couldn't have been Cam. He wouldn't announce himself.

I slid my feet across the shag carpet until I reached the door. "Who is it?" I quietly asked, still a little groggy from my slumber.

"It's Cherry." Her voice quivered.

I pulled the door open with force. "What's wrong?"

"Your grandmother has gone missing. Cam was able to track you by your chip and verify your whereabouts with staff. I'm sorry, Mrs. Marry but you understand we are not permitted to lie to Mr. Rosenthal." She nervously shook.

"Yes, yes, of course. What about my grandmother?" I didn't care about anything else at the moment.

"Somehow her device has been tampered with, they can see the general area she's located but cannot pinpoint it exactly. She's here in Charlotte!" Cherry picked at her fingernails with her head held down.

"Do you know where Cam is?" I asked.

"He, Rayan and Wesley should be arriving here momentarily." She answered my question and then scurried down the steps like a little mouse, even her behavior seemed odd.

I sat alone in the quiet and wondered where she could be. Her only connection to Charlotte is me. I went and changed into something more athletic, I was willing to hike, climb, swim, whatever it took to find her.

Did she become angry and leave as I did. That's not the way she typically handled things, but I would start there. I went from room to room, looked in every closet, crawl space, any area large enough to hold a person. I came up empty handed.

I walked down to the creek, crossed the steel pipe, and even waded through the water down both sides to be sure she was nowhere in the area. My grandmother knew what that creek meant to me, that it was always my place of solace. I hoped for one moment that maybe she had come here looking for the peace of mind that I always found in this haven. I stopped and let the wind blow through my hair. This time of year, reminded me so much of the day I met Cam nearly nine years ago. I was amazed at how far we had come but I was also saddened by the loss of mystery and desire that was once ever so present in our relationship. I guess there is a time of mourning in every love story. We long for the past flatteries and end up missing out on the present ones, never realizing how good life is for the moment.

    I looked up at the sky, trying to block the sun from my vision. The bunker! The thought took over my mind. She's got to be in the bunker. I walked in that direction, progressing to a run. An overwhelming feeling of her presence came over me.

    I ran towards the door that led beneath the barn to the bunker. It was genius how this rustic wooden structure led to something more sinister, a luxury hideout for vampires.

    The stale smell from the straw I kicked up took my breath away, but I kept to the task. I could feel the pull becoming stronger and stronger. I slowed my pace and softly walked over to the large metal door that covered the steps leading down into the shelter. I silently turned the handle and used all my strength to open the entry way. I maneuvered sideways down the steps so I could see every inch of the place, trying not to make a sound. I was very familiar with this bunker.

    There was no one in the living area when I made it to the bottom. I circled around, securing all sides. A noise from the bedroom hall broke my concentration. I followed the muffled sound until I reached the last door on the right, the room that originally belonged to Cam. I believed it was my grandmother trying to speak. I decided then that I was going in no matter what the outcome may be. I burst through the door and there she was tied to a chair, her mouth duct-taped shut.

"Shhhh." I said. I removed the seal from her mouth reminding her that we may not be alone and then I untied the thick ropes that held her to the seat. I whispered to her that everything would be okay.

Her eyes widened; her facial expression changed as she looked towards the door that secured her hostage place. "Marry, behind you!" Just that quick I was now being held along with my grandmother.

I couldn't tell much about our captor except that he was hidden behind a black mask. I figured him to be a man because of his build, he was short in stature but broad. He surveyed the room, looking for something to silence us with.

"Why are you doing this?" I asked.

"Whatever has caused this, I'm sure we can figure it out and come to some kind of agreement. Is it money you want? We can get you money!" I yelled.

"Shut up, Marry!" He kicked the door frame, stubbing his toe and then hopping around on one leg until the pain subsided. He wasn't very smart of a man, that much was for sure.

"Marry, what I want and need, you cannot give me." He huffed and puffed still searching for something to hush me with.

"I want my family back, you stupid…." He said, unable to get his sentence out before grandmother intervened.

"Watch your mouth now, son." Grandmother spoke.

He reared back and let his hand swipe across her face. I jumped up and down in the chair causing it to scoot across the floor, intending to pay him back for his abuse.

"I'll let you sit here and think about all of this." He said before he left the room, slamming the door behind him.

I couldn't understand why Cam hadn't shown up yet. He had a tracking device in me and unless it malfunctioned, there was no reason for his tardiness.

The kidnapper wasted no time coming back in the room. He flung the door open letting it bounce off the wall. Grandmother and I both flinched in fear of another altercation. He removed his mask and walked towards me with a gold handled hunting knife.

"Jon!" I screamed. I warned Cam of this and now it was all beginning to make sense.

Jon wanted his family back. Jon was my best friend Maggie's, brother, the girl that my own vampire father killed when we were teens. Her death changed my life, my father nearly destroyed me. My mother was now deceased because of his actions and up until recently, I believed he too was dead.

I was shocked to find him locked in a dungeon beneath grandmother's house, he and some of the other law-breaking vampires were placed into furnace-like cells and were being injected with animal membrane so they could withstand heat and fire. The idea was to form them into weapons should a war of vamps ever break out.

Jon had motive; his father passed away after years of scrutiny, being blamed for a car wreck that left him the prime suspect in a man's death. The deceased was my father when he was still human and after the crash almost took his life - Cam changed my father as a favor to Rayan because my dad was Rayan's stepson. But, why now? Why was Jon retaliating now and why my grandmother? She didn't have anything to do with any of this.

"Well, you know, Marry. I've got so much hate in me and for many reasons. I mean y'all come in here - into this community like you own the place. You build gigantic houses in the middle of quiet neighborhoods, I guess, in an attempt to make the rest of us feel weak or insufficient. But we're not, Marry." Jon rattled off some really harsh words.

Cam assured me we would not have any problems here. I couldn't understand why this was happening now.

"Jon, that's not at all what we're trying to do. I was raised in this neighborhood. You know that. I would've never done anything to hurt any of you and definitely not Maggie, she was my best friend. What is it that you want me to do, Jon?" I asked.

"I want you to right your wrongs." He said as he began to move closer to us.

"Neither me or my grandmother have done anything wrong." I said.

He raised his knife and darted towards my grandmother. Before either of us could let out a scream, Rayan came flying in. He swallowed Jon up with his mighty vampire stature and held him there suspended in the air. Cam was a milli-second behind Rayan. He hurried to my side. I motioned for him to release grandmother from her restraints, first. He obliged.

Grandmother stood up and straightened her blouse like the classy woman she was.

Cam tore through my rope, releasing me. He held me tightly in his arms. I was unimpressed by his heroism, he gets me into these situations and then saves me, there's nothing special about that – not anymore. Our eyes locked, he ungripped me and went to Rayan's side. The brothers took Jon and moved deeper into the bunker, down a set of steps that I never knew existed. I moved closer to the staircase. I could see the darkness and feel the damp cold coming from below.

Cam looked back towards me. "No more worries about this one. He will remain secluded in this dungeon until I decide if he should live or die." Cam spat towards Jon, pushing him down before slamming the metal door and latching it.

We all left together, Rayan carried grandmother on our trip back up to the house, not too many words were spoken.

I leaned over and politely whispered to Cam that he better not try and carry me. I was still quite angry about our unnecessary time spent with Jon. He stopped walking and gave me a blank stare before lifting me up anyways.

"You don't tell me how to handle my own wife." He growled in my ear. I felt his hot breath against my skin, wiping it away, I cringed on the inside.

"Brother, he's dealing with someone. He knows more than he should, and he's no longer transfixed. It must be VAM. There's no doubt in my mind. He's out for revenge, we must keep him locked up until we figure out who he's got working with him." Cam said.

Rayan agreed.

Cam sat me on the sofa next to where Rayan had placed grandmother.

"Please stay with me for a few days." I asked her.

"We will both stay." Rayan answered.

Cam and I both nodded, pleased with their responses.

I excused myself from the room and went back to our quarters. I figured it wouldn't be long before Cam made his way up, too. I convinced myself that I would hold on to the anger I was feeling no matter what tactic he used to try and sway me back to his side.

I slid into my comfy cotton pajamas, the ones that read, *my favorite past time is sleep.* Sleep, which I rarely got around here. I climbed into bed and flipped through the T.V. channels.

It's amazing how much crap we all go through in such a short period of time. Just this morning I was in Memphis with my family. We went to see Skylar, found him half dead and his bodyguard deceased, was left by my own husband, his brother, and the lead vampire of his group. I took a flight back to Charlotte – caught wind that my grandmother was missing, found my grandmother, got abducted with my grandmother, and then rescued by two of the three that left me alone in Memphis. I'm exhausted!

I quickly dozed off. A clear vision of Maggie formed in my mind; she began to speak to me, but I couldn't make out her words. She stood in a dark tunnel: she looked exactly like she did when I found her dead body. Her hair was healthy, cascading down her back. But the rest of her was zombie-like, frightening.

"Marry" She called out. "I'm not here to harm you. I just need you to listen." She said.

I tossed and turned, rolling from one side of the bed to the other but I couldn't wake myself.

"I have forgiven those who harmed me. I'm no longer bitter or scared. Marry!" Her voice raised, leaving me still and silent. "I am only here to tell you that you are in danger."

I didn't need Maggie to come back from the dead and tell me that, I was quite aware. I reached out for Cam, but he wasn't to be found, leaving me all alone once again. I felt the tears begin to roll down my face.

"Marry, please just listen." Maggie spoke again. "I don't have much time before I am allowed into the New Jerusalem, I have a mansion there, Marry." Her voice lightened. I could hear the excitement.

Even in my sleep, I could feel my heart aching for Cam, the need for him next to me was taking over my every being. I grabbed hold of the bed sheet and held myself steady so I could focus solely on Maggie's words.

"Jon is there to harm you all! He has formed an alliance with one member of VAM. Hear me, Marry. He is conspiring with only one single VAM. This Vampire is young and goes by the name of Tuck. Tuck has the power to be out in the daylight and that's what's keeping him safe once he and Jon commit their wicked acts. He's strong, but I have no doubt he can be taken out by any of your three - alone. You must stop them before they do something that cannot be fixed. Please, I'm begging you. I want to go to my new home in peace, with no worries." She pleaded with me.

I woke up gasping for air! I let go of the sheets, jumped

up, ran into the bathroom, and put a cold, wet rag to my face. That was the one thing mother always suggested I do when I felt myself spiraling into an anxiety attack.

I held onto the countertop and leaned over the sink. I took many deep breaths until my panic was under control. I turned to go back to bed, finding myself face to face with Cam. He appeared so quickly, I screamed, unsure of who I was looking at. I ran past him and jumped up on the bed, hopping around like a child. I looked down and warned him not to take another step forward. I grabbed the lamp off my nightstand, intending to knock him upside the head should he get any closer to me. It still hadn't registered who he was. My Maggie dream was so vivid that I found myself in a state of delusion.

Cam didn't speak a word, allowing me to continue with my rant. Cam held his hands in front of him, ready to block any move I decided to make.

"Marry!" Rayan ran through the door and grabbed me from the bed. I recognized him right away.

I put my head on his shoulders and wrapped my arms around his neck. I could no longer contain my tears." Rayan held me tight.

"Brother, go downstairs. I need to talk to you." Rayan spoke angrily towards Cam.

Rayan sat with me for a little while until he felt comfortable leaving me alone. "Are you okay, sweetheart?" He asked.

"I think so." I didn't know what else to say. I wasn't sure either way.

He tucked me in bed just like a father would. "Cam will be up shortly. He and I need to have a heart to heart or lack thereof." Rayan calmly laughed. "If you need anything, call for me." He concluded our conversation.

Once I was sure he had left the room, I got up, walked softly across the floor, quietly opened my door, and went and sat on a step near the bottom, I needed to clearly hear their words.

"Cam, what's going on?" Rayan said. "You treat your wife as if she doesn't exist. I have seen you on numerous occasions put yourself or others above her and that's unacceptable. You chose her, Cam! She didn't come looking for you as such a young girl! You manipulated her young heart into falling for you. Wasn't it real? It seemed real to me, brother." When Rayan finished speaking, a quiet lingered.

"All she really wants is for you to acknowledge her and lately, you haven't been doing that. Tell me what you're thinking?" Rayan said.

I felt a knot form in my stomach when he asked that. I wasn't sure I wanted to hear the answer, but I had to. What if he didn't love me anymore.

"Look Rayan, I'm a vampire. I can't always play the Romeo role like you do. I love her and I want to be with her, but I refuse be all lovey-dovey twenty-four, seven." Cam said. "And while you and Wesley think I don't know he asked you to take over second in command, to ex me out of my position, please believe, I am quite aware. I also know that you refused, which I appreciate. The whole fact the conversation was had, let's me know I'm not who I should be to my fellow EVG's. I will tell you this much, though. I'm not lacking in anything. I got heart, strength, and skill. You may be older than me, but I can pass any test." Cam said.

I was shocked at Wesley's actions, but I trusted Rayan would never hurt Cam.

Rayan spoke up. "It's not about strength or any skill and since you've let your pride flare up – I'll tell you this much, whoever told you about that occurrence is not part of this team and I promise you they will be abolished from this group once I find out. See, what you don't know, brother is that before we left Memphis, Wesley apologized for even asking me to solely occupy the second rank position. He assured me he would never do anything like that to you, barely remembering the talk he had with me. He swore it was because of the medical condition he was experiencing. That man isn't lying to me, Cam. I love you. Do you doubt that my brother?" Rayan said.

Cam responded, stating that he believed Rayan.

"Then go fix things with Marry, make that right. You didn't wait for her all those years to leave her up in her bedroom, crying. Make her happy. She comes first - vampire or not, love is what keeps any being alive. Find that love that used to burn so deep within you. That's what makes you who you are, Cam. Look at Read, He holds our mother's love close to his heart and finds himself content with memories and a book. Take your peaceful place back, Cam. Love that which loves you - everything else will just return void." Rayan said.

His words cut me deep. There were things I needed to change about myself, too. I only hoped Cam felt the same.

"Before you leave, let me say this. When you're ready, come to me and tell me who brought the ugliness of what appeared to be a betrayal on Wesley's part, to your attention. We cannot tolerate such manipulation. They used simple words to distract you and now me from what matters." Rayan spoke with intelligence and care towards Cam.

Dang, I love Rayan! What would we do without him? I can't help but wonder.

Realizing their conversation was over, I scurried up the steps, opened the door, jumped back in bed, pulled the covers over my head, and pretended to be asleep.

I had a feeling Cam would appear quickly. And just like that I heard the bedroom door open, the CD changer close and that old R&B started to play.

I felt him near me. He removed the covers from my body and held out his hand, I shied away which only invited him closer. He gently took my wrist and pulled me up next to him. The warmth from his face was odd, something I rarely experienced. He was blushing.

The music played on as he danced me to the middle of the room. We swayed back and forth holding one another tightly. Something unexplainable happened that night, no words were spoken but we fell deeper in love.

CHAPTER 9

We both slept into the afternoon, needing the rest. There had been so much going on lately that we neglected ourselves and each other.

We got into the shower and let the water pour over our bodies. He appeared to me as everything a man should be. I ran my hands across his muscular shoulders and down his back, lathering him in soap until I noticed blood begin to pool on the shower floor. Confused, I looked to Cam for answers. He shook his head and smiled.

"There's nothing funny about this and where is the blood coming from?" I asked.

He turned sideways revealing bruising and stitches that had been placed in the crease of his pelvic area.

"What happened there and why didn't your body heal itself?" I asked.

"Dr. Patak wants the place to stay open, so he doesn't have to slice me up repeatedly. He filled it with a certain compost yesterday and gave me an ointment to keep it from healing too quickly. The slower the process, the more likely the treatment will work." He looked me directly in the eyes while speaking.

"What are you talking about? Are you okay?" I said, nearly in tears, worried about his well-being.

"Marry, the procedure was done in order to take my seed and adjust its contents, removing the vampire DNA by inserting a filter that he created himself. This also allows for my human DNA to grow and flourish into a worthy specimen. Baby, He's in the vampire reproduction business – We must let him do his thing." Cam said while allowing himself to laugh.

I could tell he was a little anxious about the whole thing.

"The blood is normal, just a bit of me seeping out." He said.

I cringed at the thought.

"This is what we talked about. This is me doing my part to create the child that we want. The child that will be human, loved, and carefree. He should be able to test it again by next week." Cam said.

It saddened me even though I knew he was doing all of this for us. I would've been perfectly fine had he chosen not to have children, but he made it blatantly clear that he desired a child with everything in him.

I put my hand over the wound and kissed him. "What is in the compost exactly?" I asked.

"Some things are better left unknown. I'm making a choice to trust the doctor." He laughed again. "The fertilizer will help my seed take when it's implanted into you, bringing forth a better chance of pregnancy with no complications or added vampire commodities."

I could see the happiness on his face at the thought of me carrying his child - our child. Chills of excitement began to cover my body.

He wrapped his towel around me, carrying me from the shower to the bed. I laid my head on his chest and wiped the water from his naked body with my hand.

"Cam, where is Wesley?" I asked. "Cherry told me yesterday that you, Rayan, and Wesley were all three heading back to Charlotte? I haven't seen Wesley."

"Things got really hectic in Memphis yesterday. Once Skylar was settled into another room - the only way for him to heal quickly enough to survive his injuries was for Wesley to once again give of himself. I can't lie, I disapproved of this as did Rayan, but Wesley wouldn't have it any other way. I know it sounds awful, but Rayan and I would have both preferred for Skylar to go to his final death before taking more from Wesley. He's been sick since birth, living in a hospital is no life at all for that child." Cam said.

I agreed with him, but there was still the possibility of Skylar being healed. He could live a typical life if he could just get DNA replacement from a member of VAM. I wanted to tell Cam this. Wesley was killing himself by continuing to give his matter to Skylar. I just wasn't sure what would happen if I broke Wesley's trust.

"How long will Wesley have to stay in the hospital, now?" I asked.

"At least another week, he's prolonged his stay." Cam said.

It was clear to me that Wesley was troubled. You can't lead a group if you're constantly trying to save everyone in it. You appoint people to handle different circumstances and then you manage those individuals. In my heart I felt this would be Wesley's downfall. But I would never speak those words.

"Let's just stay in this bed all day." Cam fell backwards on the bed causing me to land on top of him.

"Okay." I said. I rolled over to face him. He moved my hair back away from my forehead, our eyes locked.

"What's going to happen now, Cam? Who do you think wanted to harm Skylar and kill Mike?" I asked. I felt the discussion must be had.

A frown formed on his face. "I'm not sure. I have my suspicions but for now I'm keeping those to myself. I would hate for a rumor of this magnitude to get started." He sighed.

I knew he was right.

Since we were catching up on all the recent activities, I figured I could address the Jon situation. Maybe Cam would want to hear about the dream I had right after Jon's capture.

"Cam, when I came to bed after you and Rayan put Jon in the dungeon that I knew absolutely nothing about, I had the strangest but realist dream." I said jokingly.

Cam looked at me and grinned. "I can't tell you all of my secret hiding places. What would I do if I needed to chain you up? You know you get all kinds of out of control on me sometimes." He didn't laugh but surely, he was kidding.

"Tell me about your dream, my dear." He said.

It warmed my heart that he was once again calling me by a term of endearment.

"Maggie came to me in my dream. She told me she had found forgiveness while waiting to transition to the grander side of things. She also said that Jon was evil and out for revenge, like you suggested. She mentioned that he is working with a single VAM, no more, no less, just one. His name is Tuck and he's a day walker. He's young, smart, and strong. They've been plotting together for quite some while." I was surprised at the amount of attentiveness Cam was showing me. It was then I realized my dream was factual and not just a nightmare.

"What else did she say, Marry?" Cam asked.

He took a strand of my hair and curled it around his forefinger while trying to keep a straight face as if our conversation wasn't troubling. I could feel that his nails were growing by the way my hair tangled around them. I pulled back a little way from him while continuing to speak.

"She said we really needed to stop him before things get out of hand and that she couldn't gain her reward until this was over. She wants to go to paradise in peace. But what I can't understand is why would this individual VAM want to work with lowly Jon on anything?" I posed the question to Cam to see where his mind was at.

"That's easy, Marry. After Jon's internship a few years ago at the police station, he was finally hired full time as an officer. I didn't tell you any of this because I didn't feel the need to worry you about past issues. My people at the precinct have kept an eye on him and it turns out he is participating in, if not the leader of a human trafficking ring. That's another reason Rayan and I chipped you and Elizabeth. We knew he had some mental issues, but we never thought he would take it as far as he did yesterday." He said.

I stared at him blankly, finding it hard to take all of this in but then it got worse.

"The EVG's had his operation halted immediately once it was realized exactly what type of forbidden abuse was going on. To be exact, he was smuggling children over the border and then selling them. I will not elaborate on this subject." He said.

I quickly got up from my seat. "Why?" I screamed.

"He was making millions off this and it's safe to say that Tuck benefited equally." He said.

"Jon may be hurt about his family and losing his sister and father but trust me it's nowhere near the hurt he is feeling by losing all that income. Tuck and Jon are feeling the pressure. Tuck maybe worse than Jon – When Jon is charged with human trafficking, and he will be, he will get prison time. When VAM is hit with the type of disgrace that Tuck is bringing - He will be killed. His final death is upon him. He's going to try and do everything in his power to harm me and my family. What happened to you and Elizabeth yesterday should not have been allowed to happen. I have since put extra eyes on you both." He hissed.

"This is why I hate my father, not because of the backlash we're getting but because he killed a child, my best friend and I don't care what happens to him in that fiery furnace you have him locked in!" I cried out.

I didn't realize I was still standing until Cam gently guided me back down, pulling my legs under his body and then maneuvering to look into my eyes.

"You have nothing to fear. Everyone involved in this scheme will be handled accordingly. I want us to live a peaceful life, focusing on each other and family. The time is coming." He said.

He leaned over and kissed the tip of my nose. My heart

skipped a beat, scared he was going to leave me alone again. Instead, he sat up, leaned back, and allowed himself to sink down into his seat. He motioned for me to come closer.

I jumped when someone knocked at our door.

"Who is it?" Cam yelled towards the entryway.

"Rayan. You okay in there?" He asked.

Cam and I laughed.

"Do you need something?" Cam asked.

"I'm not standing here for my health. I need to talk to you both." Rayan said.

Cam looked at me and sighed. He tossed my house coat towards me so I could cover the less than appropriate night gown I had slipped into. I tied the string and sat down.

"How do you want to handle Jon?" Rayan asked.

"You came up here for that?" Cam asked. "Just leave him there. We can interrogate him tomorrow and then decide on how we want to proceed." Cam spoke authoritatively, giving me butterflies.

"Brother, before you go, let Marry share with you the dream she had. I think it holds some significance." Cam said.

I repeated the story.

"We might have a fight on our hands, Tuck knew we would come for them about those children. I figured he would let all this go once the word was out, you know, to save himself. Makes me think Jon's holding something over his head, otherwise he wouldn't have the gumption to participate in any ill activity towards EVG." Rayan said.

After Rayan finished speaking, he departed back down the steps.

I could see the moon shining through a tiny opening in the curtain. It was after midnight by now.

"Let's go for a ride." Cam suggested.

I shrugged, wanting to be anywhere that Cam was, and

at any time.

He pulled the Mercedes around to the front of the house, the one he gave me in high school. He knew it was my favorite out of all the cars we owned.

"Let's drop the top and take in the night air. There's a little place I want to show you." He said.

We pulled out of the driveway and then away from the neighborhood. He held my hand softly, rubbing his thumb over mine. His romantic gestures reminded me of the road trips before marriage, the special times we shared alone.

The houses became tiny specks in the rearview, the cool breeze led us to the countryside. We entered Mecklenburg County, still in Charlotte but consisting mostly of farmland. The place was tranquil, off the beaten path. We turned and headed down a long, once gravel driveway, most of the rocks were spread out on its edges, dirt rumbled underneath our tires.

A small quaint farmhouse made of white painted wood appeared from behind a couple of monstrous trees, still possessing leaves. Two rickety rocking chairs sat on the front porch, a torn screen door was the only entrance into the house as far as I could tell.

A flood light buzzed above us. The moon was bright reflecting off what I knew to be a giant metal silo placed out in the field. Cam's expression went from joy to sadness in a matter of seconds. I placed my hand on his.

"This was your home?" I said.

"Born and raised." He forced a crooked grin.

He had brought me to the place where he and Rayan took on their vampire identities, Rayan after suffocating in the Silo waiting on his lover and Cam after being shot by his father in an attempt to keep him from killing their mother. The place where their father committed suicide and where Read had finessed their mother, the original cause of the change. I wondered if he considered this his personal hell or if he thought about it at all. All the sad stories he shared with me but still there was something mesmerizing about this place.

Cam walked around to my side, opening the door for me.

"How do you feel about being here?" I asked.

"I feel good. I have no regrets. If it weren't for this place and the tragic events that unfolded here, I wouldn't be the man I am today, and I wouldn't be your husband."

He picked me up, I held tightly to his bulky shoulders as we flew towards the house, coming to a landing on the worn front porch.

He placed me down near the door, taking my hand, he led me inside. We stopped after only a few steps.

"Does someone live here? Is it okay for us to be inside the house?" I asked.

Cam laughed at my question. "The property belongs to me. I bought Rayan out of his half years ago. He never liked the place, I feel differently. I have intentions of remodeling it, possibly building a much larger home a few acres back. With everything that's gone on, I feel as though we will not remain in our current home. I want the safest place possible for us to raise our family with no regrets. We will see where time leads us." He smiled and I smiled back.

"Back here." He said, taking my hand in his once again. "This is the room Rayan and I shared and across the hall is where our parents slept." He explained.

The house was a lot smaller than it looked on the outside. There was a kitchen, a living room with an old wood burning stove and a bathroom. The place seemed odd, seeing as what we were now accustomed to. I couldn't visualize Cam or Rayan living in such. If you didn't know their story, you couldn't imagine the horrific events that unfolded here.

A creepy feeling caused my arm hairs to stand up. I was glad when we finally stepped back outside.

"Can I see inside the silo?" I don't know what possessed

me to ask such a question. Wearily, he agreed.

We made our way through the tall grass, Cam gasped for more breath the closer we got.

"Let's go back." I said.

"Are you sure?" He asked.

I nodded and once again found myself flying through the air with my husband. I felt like I could reach out and grab the moon.

"Maybe this wasn't such a good idea after all." He whispered. His straight black hair fell into his face as he slightly hung his head. I reached up and gently brushed it away.

"I think it was perfect, every moment spent with you is amazing." I said.

We embraced before getting back into the convertible.

"Was that your stomach?" Cam asked after my tummy let out a rumble.

I laughed. "I'm starving. I just realized I haven't eaten all day." I said.

His disappointment appeared in the form of a frown.

He whipped the Benz over into the parking lot of a strategically placed small convenient store. He stepped out of the car and opened the door for me as he always did.

"I could have done that, you know." I laughed.

He let his fangs pop out giving me a grin and then a fifty-dollar bill so that I could make my snack purchase.

"I'll be back before you can miss me." I said. It was hard for me not to ask if he wanted anything, his diet often slipped my mind.

The bell on the store entrance let out a ding when I opened the door. I turned back to the car and simply waved at Cam. The clerk was a tall, extremely skinny guy, probably in his mid to late twenties. Politely, he asked how my night was going and complimented me on my car. It was a wonder he could see anything, his dirty blonde hair hung over his eyes. His wrinkled clothing did its best to cover up his badly blemished skin. He appeared oily from sweat and a lack of bathing. An uneasy feeling came over me.

I grabbed a coke and headed towards the chip aisle. I stared for a moment before going with the bag of Funyuns. I was amazed by all the new junk food that covered the shelves. It had been ages since I was last in a store of this caliber.

The door chimed again. I figured I was taking too long, and that Cam had come to scold and retrieve me. I looked over my shoulder only to realize it wasn't Cam. A man wielding a shotgun, his face covered by an orange ski mask, cocked his gun back and yelled for the cashier to open the register drawer. I ducked down on all fours, praying I hadn't been seen. I crawled to the edge of the display and peeped around the corner to see if Cam was aware of the horror taking place in here. My head dropped when I didn't see the car. Cam was gone!

I started to panic, taking three deep but quiet breaths, I knew I had to save myself. I turned around, sat on the floor, and positioned my back against the racks. There was a circular mirror placed in the corner of the ceiling, I watched closely as the events unfolded.

The clerk raised his hands high in the air while the thief positioned his gun right at his head. Before I could cover my eyes to prevent witnessing a killing, the cashier fell to the ground in slow motion as if someone had picked him up and laid him down.

The robber's mouth opened as his gun flew out of his hands, landing on the floor in the back of the store. The man was in a trance, unable to move. I couldn't fathom what was going on here.

I crawled over to the weapon and brought it back to my hiding spot. When I looked back at the mirror, the criminal's body was savagely being torn apart. Blood covered every inch of the counter.

"Cam?" I softly called for him. How stupid could I have Been, not to remember he hadn't a reflection.

"Don't speak until I have cleared the building. Wait here." Cam said.

He went to the back office and destroyed the security footage before lifting me up to carry me out.

"Cam, take me with you." A shaky voice called out from behind the check-out area. His look of desperation saddened me while confusion sunk in.

"Why do you know him?" I asked Cam. He left my question unanswered.

Cam tossed the clerk the keys to the old farmhouse. "You stay in my house and get yourself cleaned up, all the way up! Get it together and make sure you show up to this job every time you're scheduled. On the days you aren't working, take that time to paint and fix up my place. I'll bring you some supplies tomorrow. Don't let me ever see you looking this raggedy again, understood?" Cam said in an irritated but demanding tone.

The guy shook his head up and down, agreeing with Cam's every word.

"It's obvious you owed this jokester some money and that's why he came in here with this foolishness but don't let my niceness confuse you. I want to make this much clear, had something happened to my wife, you would've died your last death, baby boy." Cam said to the man.

"I promise, Cam! I won't let you down, man." The cashier spoke while he reached to pick up the keys Cam had thrown to him. His hands unsteady but he managed to get a grip on them.

Cam looked back towards him one last time. "Don't let yourself down." Cam said.

CHAPTER 10

"When I looked out the window, you were gone. I thought you left me." I said as tears began to form in my eyes. I gasped for my next breath.

"Calm down, my dear. You are okay and you should know by now, I will never leave you." He said. "You've been in more dangerous situations than that one." He smiled. "I hadn't gone anywhere. I recognized the truck pulling in the lot and then, I realized who was working in that store. I put two and two together, pulled the car around to the side, out of view. I went in directly behind that lowlife. He just never knew it. I even gave him the benefit of the doubt, hoping no drama ensued. Unfortunately, things took a turn for the worse."

Cam was my personal superhero. His features were so outlined after an altercation bringing out even more of his beauty. I leaned over to kiss him, realizing he was covered in blood.

He shook his head. "Don't. I must get cleaned up first. You must stay healthy, my love. There are tainted bloods in this cruel world and I wish for you never to encounter them."

"Why did you give him keys to your farmhouse, Cam?" I asked.

"Our farmhouse, we are one." He said.

"The short story is this, Sharon…." He said.

I immediately stopped him.

"Why does everything have to involve her?" I asked. I could feel my face heat up with anger.

"Look, you either want the story or you don't and as much as I wish it didn't involve Sharon, it does." He said. He bugged his eyes towards me. I balled my fist up, wishing I could punch something or someone!

"Okay, tell me." I said.

"Sharon was in her early thirties when she was changed

to EVG. She and her brother, the cashier at the store, were nearly killed in a car crash about three miles back from here. It was a crucial time for the vampire race. Everyone was trying to get the most members until finally we called a truce, agreeing to only change humans that we desired and wanted to heal, not just for numbers." Cam said.

The car swerved to the left avoiding a large stone that was littering the roadway.

"Cam!" I screamed.

"That would have flattened your tire and possibly bent a rim." He shrugged.

"Both were nearly lifeless. Read was at the farmhouse unbeknownst to any of us, rendezvousing with my mother, I'm sure. Please know that this is confidential information for Skylar's sake and because Sharon must always be looked upon as Wesley's daughter." He said.

"Of course." I responded, not sure what any of this had to do with Wesley's parental status.

"The leader of VAM, Shelton, was also nearby. Read flew to the scene in an attempt to multiply our kind, he was successful in changing Sharon but her brother, Stevie, was changed by Shelton. I know how crazy this all must sound." He laughed.

It was no crazier than everything else in my fairytale life. I chuckled on the inside.

He continued. "Stevie has been in a bad way with drugs for some time and a lot of his decisions lack moral understanding. VAM exiled him rather quickly because of this. They tried working with him to help him get his life in order and cooperate with the VAM way, but it was pointless. His senses and strength amounted to nothing because of his substance use which rendered him garbage to his newfound group. He couldn't feed off humans, their blood made him sick. He lives off dope and the occasional animal carcass which only weakens him more. He's just a replica of a human. I feel bad for him because I know his struggle is real. In my eyes he's still a kid and if I can be of help to him then I feel I must do so." He said.

It was times like this that made me fall deeper in love with my husband. I chose to just listen.

"He cannot steal anything of value from me nor can he harm that old house. I don't think he would if he could. His time is near. He's got to regroup, or he will no longer exist. I've heard stories of what VAM plans to do to him – He is a disgrace to their kind." Cam said.

The night air was getting cooler. He must've noticed me rub my uncovered arms. He slowed his speed, allowing the top to close on the vehicle.

"They're going to kill him, Cam?" I asked.

"Sooner or later, Marry, and probably sooner than later." His tone lowered.

"Could there be any repercussions for you helping him?" I asked.

"No, his state keeps away strife. I have put him to work and maybe if he detoxes there, VAM will reconsider his membership." He said.

Cam was good even though he couldn't always let that side of him show.

"How does Sharon feel about her brother being VAM?" I asked.

"I'm sure she still has love for him, she's always wanted him to get better so that one day he could work on the Children's hospital research team with her. It's just one of those things that no one ever talks about. I don't know what their relationship is like now." He said.

I was so bewildered by everything that occurred tonight; I didn't realize we were now sitting in the driveway of our own home.

"Come on, my dear. Let's go inside so we can get cleaned up. I might as well carry you; it appears I have already gotten blood on you." He said.

He lifted me and took me directly up to the bath.

The sun was going to rise in less than an hour. I needed rest.

"Where are you going?" I asked, half asleep. I became fully aware after he kissed me on the forehead and began to tiptoe away.

"Rayan and I have business to tend to. Jon still needs to be dealt with. We need to figure some things out. Your grandmother is downstairs, no need to worry my love, no need to worry at all." He blew me a fangy kiss as he left the room.

CHAPTER 11

Grandmother, Cherry, and I sat in the living room sharing stories of when we first met, the laughs seemed endless. I missed my mother terribly.

"What do you want to do, brother? Call in the paramedics?" The front door caught a gust of wind and slammed closed behind the two brothers.

Cam laughed. "What'd you jump for? Think someone was chasing you?" He asked Rayan.

"I wish they would." Rayan replied.

Cam walked over to me, pretending not to see me, and purposely sat on top of me. "Oh, pardon me, miss. I didn't realize anyone was sitting here." He said jokingly.

"I can't stand you!" I said, we both laughed and then shared a quick kiss.

Cam looked towards Cherry. "Hello, do you mind leaving the room for a moment? My family and I must discuss some things." He said.

She obliged.

We all thought highly of Cherry. She was a wonderful help.

Rayan slid down next to grandmother, kissing her on the way which turned into a next level smooch, causing me to cover my eyes and cringe.

"Make them stop, Cam." I said in disgust.

Cam cleared his throat. "Oh, to be young and in love." Cam said, laughing.

Rayan pulled back from grandmother, raised his eyebrows, and then shrugged.

"Okay, we thought you would be interested in knowing what's going on with Jon." Rayan said.

"I, for one am interested seeing as you both came in the house talking about calling the EMT's." I said.

"What's EMT, Marry? A new vampire group?" Grandmother asked.

We joined one another in laughter.

Cam chimed in "We've been questioning Jon all morning trying to figure out his motivation for the kidnappings, trying to see where his mind is at, or even if he has one at this point." He smiled.

"He does blame us for the loss of his sister and demise of his family unit. Truthfully, the way his daddy sopped up the liquor, that was coming anyway. Secondly, he believes we shut down his illegal trafficking operation and yes, we did that! What we cannot understand is how he and Tuck became a team. The more we question him about this, the more unreasonable and defiant he becomes." Cam said.

"We have about a week to figure this out. We had him call his Sargent down at the precinct and explain he wouldn't be back to work until the middle of next week for reasons beyond his control. If all goes well, we'll send him back with a doctor's excuse." Rayan said.

We all laughed again.

"Sincerely, Dr. Alexander Patak." Cam added.

I felt ashamed that all this was funny to me. I did worry what would happen if Tuck showed up here and tried to rescue his business partner.

"There is something I want to make you all aware of. Last night Marry and I were down by the old Farmhouse, we stopped by the gas station for snacks." Cam said.

"Hmmmmm…" Rayan made a suspicious noise.

"No, not like that!" Cam calmed him. "Marry went in for snacks and the place was robbed at gunpoint. Stevie was the clerk and he's in really bad shape." Cam said and then hung his head.

"I was able to stop him from being physically hurt or worse and the world is now less one drug dealer. I hired Stevie to do some work for me so he's staying on the property out there. Just in case you hear anything." Cam said.

Rayan's face turned cold. "What is it about that boy? VAM didn't want him, what is it that you see in him?"

Rayan asked.

"Exactly that! He's a boy and he's lost. What boy hasn't had a hard time finding his way?" Cam replied.

"We're going to run some supplies out to him shortly." Cam said.

My grandmother spoke up "Oh Rayan, darling, it's been so long since I've been out to the old place – Let's all go, shall we?" She asked.

Even though I knew the home to be a horrible place for Rayan to revisit – He agreed. He would do anything for Elizabeth Rosenthal.

"We'll take my truck." Rayan said. "I've been looking for a reason to pull old Bessy out of the garage. We can load her up with whatever he needs." Rayan said with the biggest smile.

We all shook our heads in shame. He was speaking of a white 2003 Chevrolet Silverado with a crew cab and the biggest tires I had ever seen. None of us were accustomed to such an old mode of transportation. I wondered if I should wear my cowboy boots and a hat.

"Here goes nothing, I suppose." Cam said.

"Yep, let the games begin." Rayan taunted him with his words.

I actually loved the idea.

We loaded that truck with any and everything that would possibly fit in the back. We had to be a sight to see coming down the road, radio blaring, Rayan's arm hanging out of the window, hitting the door to every beat. Grandmother and I both sat in the back, our hair flying sporadically in the wind, coming back to smack us in the face. Cam sang loudly pretending to hold a microphone. This was the most fun the four of us had together in what seemed like an eternity.

Rayan drove right through the grass at the old farmhouse. "This truck does not need a driveway!" Rayan said as we bounced back and forth over the rough terrain.

Stevie's little car was parked in the driveway, I guess that was a good sign. He was there at least. I was anxious to go into the house - not sure what we would find.

Stevie made his way outside when Cam and Rayan began unloading the truck.

"Hey y'all, Cam." Stevie said.

He didn't seem as jittery as last night but he by no means looked any better.

Grandmother and I spoke and then Cam and Rayan went and shook the boy's hand. They were gentlemen.

"Are you working over at the store tonight?" Cam asked him.

"No sir, I'm off tonight. But I've already started working on that living room floor in there. I've pulled up some of the hardwood to replace it. I noticed some buckling in a few places, especially over by that wood stove. Come check it out." Stevie said.

"I'll wait outside." Rayan said, taking a few steps back, slightly bowing and waving his hand for grandmother and me to join Cam on the inside. Grandmother gave him a quaint smile, not making a fuss about his decision not to enter the house.

We walked across the dust covered floor. Stevie held a broom and swept before us as we moved. It was obvious he had been working. In addition to the flooring, he was in the beginning stages of removing the tacky wallpaper that was still hanging in some spots.

An old sleeping bag took up a corner of the family room, a flashlight and a cooler sat next to it.

"I will be by to check on you periodically and know that one mess up puts you out of here and I do mean just a single wrongdoing and you will be gone." Cam said.

Stevie's face straightened showing a bit of fear and understandably so.

Grandmother and I gave Stevie a subtle wave as Cam stayed back for a moment to continue their conversation.

Rayan was already in the truck, engine running. We all sat there quietly until Cam began to walk our way. He opened the back door, escorting grandmother out of the vehicle.

"My lady, will you join your husband up front for the drive home, I would like to sit next to my beautiful wife." He grinned.

My insides melted.

Cam climbed in next to me. He leaned seductively in my direction. "Why don't you and I go see the doctor in Memphis tomorrow, Marry? I feel as though my seed is ready, fatherhood must be but a short time way." He whispered. He planted a sweet kiss on my cheek.

"Let's do it." I softly spoke back. He smiled that big, beautiful smile that would make me do anything for him.

"Elizabth, pop in that old school disc. We have got to get your man out of his funk." Cam said.

Grandmother obliged and Rayan couldn't help but smile when Cam leaned up in between the seats and sang directly to Rayan. Rayan returned the love by taking the next line. They harmonized well together.

"All I think about is my baby." Cam belted that line out with a lot of force. He winked at me. I winked back.

Once home, we spent a peaceful evening alone.

"First thing in the morning, we see Dr. Patak, after we're finished there, we'll check in on Wesley and Skylar." Cam said.

The plans had been made.

CHAPTER 12

"This is something you should do as a couple. Elizabeth and I are going to hang back and I'm going to spend a little time with Jon." Rayan said. He shook his newspaper and opened it to the section he desired.

He knew where we were going without either of us saying a word.

"Are you reading the comics again, child?" Cam said trying to keep a straight face.

"Don't make me get up out of this chair, baby brother. Stay in your place." Rayan replied before both began to laugh.

"Don't do anything I wouldn't do to Jon before I get back." Cam said.

Rayan's eyes raised above the paper.

"Well, I'm just saying, if we need to kill him, let's do it together, as a family." Cam said.

"Cam." I yelled.

He scooped me up in his arms and held me there, suspended in air. "I'm sorry love, but if you put two and two together and subtract Jon and Tuck, what do we have? .... No problems!" He laughed but his expression told me he was serious.

"We still have a problem. We have yet to determine who murdered Mike and tried to take out Skylar." Rayan reminded Cam of the original killings.

"Yeah, you have a point, brother, a very large one at that! A pointy head." Cam said. He then rushed me to the car before Rayan could cast a responding insult.

We flew in Wesley's jet and then one of his drivers picked us up, escorting us to the hospital. We left our bags in the car, so I didn't feel any pressure to stay. Cam claimed the choice was all mine, but I knew differently.

Cam fixed his suite coat after he helped me out of the car, I did the same to my skirt and blouse. We must always

be presentable in public. A law clearly written in the EVG's handbook.
We walked hand in hand with our heads held high just like the power couple I believed us to be.

Cam had Dr. Patak paged as soon as we entered the hospital. There was literally no wait.

"Hello Mr. and Mrs. Rosenthal." Dr. Patak said as he reached his hand out to shake Cam's.

"Good morning, sir. Are we ready to get started? My wife and I don't wish to waste any time as we have a large agenda for today." Cam said.

I wondered if that was his real reason for rushing the doctor or if he was just so anxious that he couldn't possibly stand to wait.

"Come on back, we'll get straight to work." The doctor said and then waved us down a long, well-lit corridor. He used his badge to gain entrance into what appeared to be an operating room. The lights shined bright above two surgical tables. I became nauseous – unsure of what would happen next.

He took a chart from atop a desk and asked Cam to undress. "Put this gown on, Cam and then have a seat on the table." Dr. Patak said.

I was shocked at how well Cam took orders.

"Marry, you can have a seat over there, if you wish." He pointed to a leather chair in the corner. I backed up, nearly missing the seat when I nervously sat down.

The doctor put on some gloves, letting them plop against his wrist. He then began to exam the spot on Cam's leg in which the fertilizer had been placed. He took a pair of medical scissors and cut away at the stitches to open the wound. He pulled a swab from a jar, the metal top clinked as he replaced it. He returned to Cam's side with the long cotton topped stick. He placed it into Cam's leg and circled it around until the contents of his sore coated it. He took the specimen over to the microscope, placing it on a slide and examining it very closely. This all looked elementary to me, no big deal.

"Cam, you can redress. Marry, do you mind?" Dr. Patak said. He pointed towards the table. It was my turn. He didn't ask me to undress, taking only my temperature and vitals.

Dr. Patak's smile grew. "Do you want to give it a go? We could possibly get a baby out of this. I'm going to inject Marry with your seed and check back with you in about a week. How does that sound?" Dr. Patak directed his question towards Cam, only.

Cam's body shook, trying to hold in his excitement.

I sat quietly on the table wondering if anyone cared how I felt. I figured now was as good a time as any. At least I wouldn't have extra time to worry about it.

"I can't guarantee that this will work but I feel rather confidant." Dr. Patak said.

"Marry, please undress from the waist down, put this hospital gown on and once you are positioned, I will have my nurse come in to help you get your legs properly in the stirrups." Dr. Patak said.

Cam appeared directly over me in less than a second, his eyes glazed from happiness. He bent down and placed a gentle kiss upon my cheek. Holding my hand, he whispered. "Thank you."

I wanted to scream but instead squeezed his fingertips in affirmation.

Just as promised Dr. Patak's nurse appeared and pulled me until my bottom was all the way at the edge of the table. She did as he instructed and placed my feet into the stirrups. Dr. Patak slowly approached me with a very large syringe. I closed my eyes and held my breath.

Cam inhaled and exhaled loudly, letting out a wheezing sound. I found it better to ignore him.

"Marry, you will feel just a tad bit of pressure." Dr.

Patak said. The doctor's accent reminded me I wasn't at home.

And just like that, he was finished.

"You may get up and get dressed, dear." Dr. Patak said.

I heard the water cut on and the soap dispenser activate before he left Cam and I alone in the room.

Cam helped me off the table and once I was dressed the doctor reentered the room, handing me a prescription.

"These are prenatal vitamins that I'm nearly positive you will need." Dr. Patak said. "I will see you both back this time next week then?" He asked.

"Yes Sir." Cam said. He shook the doctor's hand as I bashfully smiled.

"I left a little something for you in an envelope over on your desk, doc." Cam said.

"Where's my little something? Don't I get a little something for my troubles?" I asked.

"You get a lot of something – All the time!" Cam said adding a wink to his statement.

He gripped my hand and looked down at me. "Let's not share what went on here today with anyone. I would rather time pass before we acknowledge a baby on the way." He seemed so sure about this which sent butterflies flickering through my tummy unless they weren't butterflies at all. I rubbed my stomach and followed his lead.

We rounded the corner to Wesley's room nearly bumping into Sarah, Benji and her security detail which had many new additions since the murders.

Sarah ran up and hugged me tightly, Benji took Cam's hand and shook it vigorously. Cam laughed.

"Well look at you Benji, you're turning into quite the strapping young man, and it's only been a week since we last met." Cam said.

Benji smiled from ear to ear. His self-esteem, increasing by the moment.

"They are supposed to release daddy today or first thing

84

in the morning." Sarah said as she clicked her heels together and jumped short of an inch off the ground. "That's why we're here. We'll stay until we can take him home." Sarah said.

Benji scooted a little closer to Cam. "Cam, I'm glad you're here, buddy. I need to talk to you for a second." Benji said. "And in private, please."

Cam raised his eyebrows towards me as the two stepped into an empty room.

I moved closer to the room to eaves drop – like always!

"Shelton is in there with Wesley." Benji said.

Before I could question in my mind why the leader of VAM would be in the hospital room with the leader of the EVG, Cam flew directly from his place into Wesley's room. I followed right behind him, unsure of what he would do. Wesley was clearly expecting Cam. He threw his hand up to halt him then Sarah's security stepped in front of Cam.

"Please excuse him, his temper has not yet mellowed." Wesley said, speaking of Cam.

"I actually thought I was being punked by these peons." Cam said. He balled his fists slightly and let out a lowly growl.

"Cam, I would like to introduce you to Shelton. He is top commander for VAM." Welsey said.

"I am aware." Cam said.

Cam moved in closer to Shelton who was sitting in the corner chair by the window. Shelton wore a three-piece black suit. His hair was as dark as his clothing and slicked back. His skin, pale just like all the other vampires around.

"To what do we owe this pleasure?" Cam said.

The situation seemed so serious, yet I felt a need to laugh. The angrier Cam got the more handsome he appeared to me.

"Shelton here, says he has some information he would like to share with us." Wesley said.

"Is that so?" Cam responded. His bad attitude still shining through.

Shelton spoke with just as much class and integrity as Wesley. He uncrossed his legs and ran his long, bony hands over his pants. "I have heard rumors of the events that unfolded here, at the hospital with your grandson Skylar and his bodyguard Mike. This visit is casual and only to let you know that I believe I have stumbled upon some information that may be of value to you and your group." Shelton said.

Cam began to open his mouth when Wesley again hushed him with his hand. The pure look of disgust on Cam's face worried me.

Shelton continued. "What I'm about to say may come as a shock to everyone in this room but I believe my knowledge to be factual and of importance, but I will not disclose my source. This individual is being monitored and dealt with accordingly to make sure there was no VAM influence which again - I believe there was not." Shelton said.

"Understood." Wesley replied.

We all anxiously waited to hear what Shelton had to say.

Shelton strangely put his hands together, the tips of his fingers touching. He turned to face Wesley and began to reveal his data. "From my understanding, your daughter, Sharon is the vampire who beheaded Mike. She seductively put him in a situation from which he could not escape. Once she rid the world of him, she went after her own son, Skylar, finding it impossible to complete the gruesome task she placed upon herself." Shelton said.

Cam placed himself quickly in front of Shelton, bypassing security with ease. Shelton looked up at Cam and smiled, crossing his legs once more, unconcerned with Cam's presence.

"I feel I must warn you that she will try again when the

opportunity presents itself and she will succeed." Shelton said.

Cam stood perfectly still, his eyes frozen on Shelton.

"Do with this information what you must as I could not watch an innocent child suffer." Shelton said.

I was dumbfounded by what I just heard. I knew that Skylar's father was a member of VAM. The odds were that Shelton spoke the truth. But why would Sharon want to kill Skylar. I couldn't understand it. Maybe to keep her secret from getting out.

Wesley immediately spoke to Cam. "Cam, I will need to speak with you privately once Shelton and the others have exited the room."

I backed out of the room but positioned myself where I could once again hear what they would say. I was getting good at secret listening.

"Thank you for your time and the courtesy you have shown us. This has not gone unnoticed." Wesley said.

"Thank you." Cam surprisingly repeated Wesley's words.

"I wish you well on your medical journey." Shelton shook Wesley's hand and then tipped his top hat.

"No journey, a quick genetic test is all, strong as ever. Volunteering ourselves for research is the best thing we can do for our groups." Wesley said as he smiled and bid Shelton adieu.

"Indeed. There is nothing I would not do for mine." Shelton said.

"I'm just thankful for my Rosenthal boys. They are the beasts behind the beast." Wesley laughed that deep, unforgettable laugh after speaking. I knew he wasn't joking! Everyone in that room knew he wasn't joking!

Shelton smiled and nodded as he walked past me sniffing the air as if something were foul.

Cam and Wesley were the only two left in the room. I

hoped Wesley would share with Cam what he had already told me.

"I believe Shelton to be of truth. I have had some intel for quite some time that I have chosen to keep quiet for the safety of the EVG's. I know this may be hard for you to hear and even harder for you to believe." Wesley said. "Come closer." He said to Cam. "Skylar is half VAM." Wesley whispered.

I could feel the air thicken from the hallway. A matter of silent moments lapsed.

"Skylar's father is VAM?" Cam finally asked.

"That's exactly what I'm saying but I don't know who the father is, yet. The doctors here picked up the VAM DNA in his blood. They immediately told me what they found, and Cam, I was just as shocked as you are now. The most disheartening part of this is the fact that had Sharon been honest to us in the beginning, Skylar could have gotten all the nutrients and transplants that he needed from a VAM member, and he wouldn't have had to live in a hospital." Wesley said.

I could hear Cam breathing, inhaling, and exhaling his anger like he had done so many times before with me.

"She must suspect that her secret is out, that's why she is trying to kill Skylar. I want him out of this place. We need to move him somewhere secure until Sharon can be dealt with." Wesley said. His voice was now louder than I had ever heard before.

"We should behead her. It's as simple as that. She can't just get away with this. It's betrayal. She has caused you unnecessary harm and has single-handedly caused that poor child to have no life whatsoever. He'll be lucky if he ever does." Cam spoke with determination.

I was all for taking Sharon out. I never liked her anyways. I gasped at my own thoughts.

"I agree with you, son. But there's more to it than this. I need her living so I can figure out who that boy's daddy is.

That just can't go unsolved for the sake of punishing her and we may need her to figure it out." Wesley said.

"She will suffer the consequences as soon as we have our questions answered. Skylar will then receive the treatment he requires. I will personally make sure that his very own father will be the one that offers himself as a sacrifice to allow Skylar to live a normal life, if we must drain and freeze the lowlife VAM." Cam said.

I knew it took everything in him to hold back his emotions and not go kill Sharon at this very moment.

"Cam, I would like to have hospital personnel bring Skylar to your home. I know that you are equipped to handle any situation. You and Rayan are by far two of the strongest and smartest vampires out there. Your women are chipped and are forever safe." Wesley said.

"We will send a trusted doctor and two nurses to stay around the clock. Do you think Marry will mind?" Welsey said.

I knew whether I cared or not was irrelevant. Cam would make the decision for us.

"She has always had Skylar's best interest at heart, and could you send Dr. Patak as the doctor? I have use for him." Cam said.

Wesley cleared his throat. "As you wish." Wesley replied, chuckling.

"Go back to Charlotte tonight and prepare for Skylar's arrival." Welsey said.

"I need to tell Marry everything or she could possibly endanger herself with the lengths she will go in order to figure out why this is happening." Cam said and then they both laughed as did I.

Cam heard my laughter. The door swung open, I jumped back and covered my mouth to prevent the array of giggles that awaited.

"How long have you been standing here?" Cam asked.

"I just walked up." I replied.

"Yeah right." He closed his eyes and held them shut for a second, shaking his head. He took me gently by the arm and brought me back into Wesley's room.

"You know she's heard all of this, don't you?" Cam asked Wesley.

"Of course, I do. But would we want her any other way?" Wesley said. His now annoying laugh carried through the air.

Cam turned to lead us back out of the room, Wesley gave me a quick wink. Our secrets were safe with one another. Cam would never know I already knew everything before today.

"Skylar will be released solely into your care. You will have the authority to make all decisions in my absence. Only your inner circle should know his where a bouts. Skylar does not recollect anything and is to remain uniformed. He shall never know what his mother attempted. That would crush his spirit. The hospital staff will be prohibited from telling his location, especially to Sharon. She has lost all rights to her son. Her lack of knowledge should send her fuming to me. I will tell her he has been quarantined for whatever reason and we'll go from there." Wesley said.

The vampire mind moves as quickly as the body.

Wesley held his forehead. "I feel like I'm leaving something out." He said.

Cam frowned, concerned about Wesley's assumed forgetfulness.

He walked back towards Wesley and took his hand. "I love you, old man." Cam said.

"Get out of here, jokester." Wesley snapped back.

The walk back to the waiting room was a quiet one.

I gave Cam's hand a squeeze. "Everything will be fine." I assured him.

"I'm going to crank the heat on the furnace as soon as we get back to Charlotte. It's time to increase the training of our soldiers. There's too much going on at once and I'm not sure what to make of it." Cam said.

My father crossed my mind for a brief second, however when Maggie entered it, she hung there longer. I could imagine my best friend still alive and living my life with me.

"Cam." Benji came around the corner. He moved so fast his shoes squealed across the freshly waxed tile. "Thank you for handling that, Cam. I wasn't sure what to do." Benji said.

"Good eye, youngster. You did right. Always speak up if something doesn't appear right. Pretty soon, you and Sarah will have to spend some time with us in Charlotte. Me and Rayan will put you up on handling some things yourself." Cam said.

Benji swung his leg up high in an attempt at a karate kick. Cam had a way of getting Benji all hyped up.

We had nearly exited when a voice came over the loudspeaker. "Cam Rosenthal, please come to the nurse's station." Puzzled, we headed back in that direction, passing by Benji once more.

"Miss me already?" Benji asked.

"No!" Cam shook his head.

"Sir, Mr. Wesley gave me this to return to you. It was left in his room." The nurse handed Cam a small, rectangular piece of paper.

"My prescription." I sighed.

"You mustn't be so careless. This is for the betterment of our child." Cam reprimanded me.

"I wish there was another exit. I'm tired and I don't feel like speaking to anyone else." I said to Cam.

"There is another exit - Anything for you, my dear." Cam said as he picked me up and took me into an empty patient room. He planted a kiss on my forehead. We flew out of the window and up four stories to the roof top.

I couldn't wait to get back home.

CHAPTER 13

"What in the world is all that noise?" I asked. The sound echoed up the steps and circled around right into my eardrum. I covered my ears.

"Movers, dear. Skylar's things have arrived." Cam said.

I looked around the room now realizing I was back at home. Apparently, I slept the entire journey.

"I wanted to help get his things situated and decorate for him." I raised my arms above my head and yawned.

"I can handle this. Didn't I do a good job on your house, huh? Didn't I?" Cam asked.

He leaned over and kissed me softly on the forehead moving my hair back away from my face. He handed me a glass of water and a large tan pill. "Take this. Doctor's orders." He said.

I examined it and forced it down my throat nearly gagging from its size.

I dozed off again, sleeping until the next morning.

I awoke with massive hunger pains. The voices coming from downstairs were different but in a familiar way. I knew our guests had arrived.

I slipped on my pink bunny house shoes that once belonged to my mother and went down to greet them, unashamed of my appearance because I hadn't the strength to dress properly.

Cam called out good morning as I made my way into the living room. He flew over, pulling me close by wrapping his arms around my waist. He backed up only a tad to strangely stare into my eyes.

Dr. Patak gave me a slight wave from his position at the kitchen table. Two female nurses sat next to him, one was quite the looker, heightening my jealous senses.

"Marry, this is Sasha and Randy, my assistants while we are here in Charlotte." Dr. Patak said.

I nodded. Sasha sounded like a name given to a street

walker and Randy, for a girl? That wouldn't have been my first choice. I stood there in a daze, sure the whole room was now aware how uncomfortable the two made me.

"Come see Skylar and his new room." Cam said, turning me around to head in the opposite direction of the medical professionals. I rolled my eyes at him. He scowled back at me. Realizing my actions, I couldn't recall a time in which I was so rude or this lacking self-confidence. I felt my grandmother's ways coming out in me but then again, even she doesn't take it to this extreme.

Cam had chosen to give Skylar my mother's old room. I felt it appropriate and hoped that it would be a sanctuary for Skylar, a place of new beginnings and happiness. The room was bright with light, the walls covered in sporadic clouds and blue skies, wallpaper so Skylar wouldn't be exposed to chemicals found in paint. Flashy jets, like Wesley's hung from the ceiling.

"Watch this, Marry." Skylar cheerfully spoke to me.

He pressed a small red button on the side of his hospital bed and all the sudden little men in parachutes fell from the ceiling. He clapped his hands together as they came down.

"Wow! That is truly amazing!" I said. It really was.

Cam stood next to me with the biggest grin on his face, almost as large as the one Skylar was wearing.

"Marry, do you see that? Look at that television hanging on the wall! It's nearly as big as my whole room back at the hospital and it has video games!" Skylar said.

Cam flopped down in a chair next to the bed, it resembled a giant hand. Air gushed from its insides as Cam's weight made contact with the seat. We all got a good laugh out of that.

"Uncle Cam can sit right there and play the games with me." Skylar said. His voice already had an influx of energy. Cam shook his head up and down, agreeing.

"He's too old for games." I said, pretending to smack Cam on the hand.

"So, is it safe to say you are going to be happy here, then?" I said.

"Yes ma'am, I'm so glad to be out of that hospital. I can't wait for my mom to come and visit me so she can see all of this." Skylar said.

My smile turned upside down.

Cam sprung from his seat. "Your mother is away on business, and I am unsure when she shall return. Maybe your father, Ken will be able to visit soon." Cam said.

It was safe to offer Ken as an alternative seeing as he couldn't possibly know about Sharon's extracurricular activities.

Dr. Patak and Sasha entered the room. Sasha wore a white miniskirt, the blouse to match and a nurse's cap with a red cross embroidered on the side. I was unaware of her scant uniform until she now stood in front of me.

"Cam, would you and Mrs. Marry mind stepping out in the hall while we check a few things? Skylar's journey here was a quick one. I want to be sure his vitals and other readings are still satisfactory." Dr. Patak said.

I didn't comprehend much of what the doctor had spoken after I was sure Sasha gave Cam, the eye, a quick subtle raise of the eyebrows and blink of the lids. I gripped Cams hand and pulled him into the hall, taking it upon myself to slam Skylar's door with vengeance.

"What is wrong with you, Marry?" Cam said. His eyes turned a bloody red, the bulging veins noticeable from inches away.

"What made anyone, or thing think it was okay to bring that hoochie in this house?" I said.

"Do you want me to let her go, Marry?" Cam said.

"Well since you know who I'm talking about without me saying her name, then yes! Absolutely let her go!" I spoke loud enough that I was sure I was heard throughout the house.

Sasha gently opened Skylar's bedroom door, keeping her

head down, and hands folded in front of her, walked past the two of us and straight to the front door. My only thoughts were that at least she was leaving without the assistance of a cleanup crew.

"Fixed! Now, what else is bothering you, my dear? I know your soul, spill it." Cam said.

"I want Jon gone. You don't have to kill him, but I need him off this property, knowing that he's here brings an uneasy feeling upon me." I told him.

"He has been well taken care of, fed and watered my love." Cam shot me a sideways grin.

"Watered?" I said.

"Yes, watered. Rayan and I will handle Jon promptly. Go get some rest." He said. He kissed my forehead before he went back into see Skylar.

CHAPTER 14

The leather sunk in when I flopped down on the sofa to watch a little television. Rarely, did I have time to enjoy such a treat though Cam referred to it as nonsense. The thought produced a grin.

The slightest tap at our bedroom door startled me. It creaked open without me agreeing to entry. "Grandmother!" I yelled. "You scared me half to death."

"Only half?" She said before laughing. "Marry, darling, they have somehow managed to let that boy, Jon, escape. He's still in the yard but now our boys and the help are out there swarming around him like a pack of bees, trying to subdue him." Grandmother said. She shook her head, shamefully. "We should probably go out there, the whole thing would be inappropriate for the neighbors to see."

I jumped up and followed grandmother out the back door. "What is this?" I said. Rayan and Cam flying around pointlessly, could have easily captured Jon by now.

Gasping, I took grandmother by the wrist. "Let's go back in. They are trying to get Tuck to respond to their actions against Jon. I can feel it. We are in danger if we remain out here." I said.

As soon as the patio door closed behind us, Tuck swooshed by and headed in Jon's direction. His ability to withstand sunlight was the only advantage he had on the brothers, luckily, Cam and Rayan had been working on strengthening themselves to tolerate sunlight for longer periods.

It all made sense. That's why Tuck never attempted to rescue Jon while he was in the bunker. He couldn't have come close to winning that battle. I knew in his small mind that somehow, he thought he could overpower Cam and Rayan in the sunlight. Tuck tried his best to prolong the situation by maneuvering himself around, but he couldn't withstand the power of Cam's force.

Cam stretched his arm out and slammed it across Tuck's face, causing Tuck to fall to the ground. He got up but was immediately forced back down with another dynamic blow from Cam.

I heard Rayan laugh. "Let it all out, baby brother. I know you've been waiting for this energy release for some time now." Rayan circled around Jon and allowed Cam to do all the fighting.

Cam leaned his upper body back and waited for Tuck to stabilize. Tuck shook his head and flew towards Cam.

A mighty gust of wind blew Rayan feet away.

Cam, full of anger and like a lightning bolt from the sky, kicked that VAM so hard that he became lodged in one of the trees that outlined the creek. Tuck's neck had been penetrated by a branch. It held him there like an ugly ornament on a Christmas tree. Cam was ferocious and so much more than that. He was my loving husband.

My grandmother turned her head to block the violent scene from her eyes. I found myself intrigued by the brutality, the crucial devastation which our husbands had brought upon the enemy. The two were true protectors.

The branch slowly pulled Tuck's head away from his neck, his body weight gave the tree no option. This would be his final death and rightfully so. I cringed at the pain and suffering cast upon children by Jon and his vampire counterpart.

Rayan's face began to flush, barely visible steam came from his ears. Grandmother noticed it quickly. "Ray." She called out. That was the first time she shortened his name in my presence.

Rayan went in for Jon, scooping him up under his arm and forcefully carrying him back to the bunker. Jon's body went limp as they entered the barn door.

Cam flew underneath the tree line. Their arms of green gave him enough protection to rebuild his tolerance for the sun. He waited for Tuck's body to fall, glancing up every second or two.

I could hear Tuck's flesh tearing from inside the house and finally a thud as his head and body bounced off the ground. Cam, refreshed, scooped his corpse up and took it to the bunker as well.

"I'm going down there." I said to grandmother.

"I beg your pardon." Grandmother replied. Her lips tightened and a scowl formed on her face. "You will do no such. We don't know if another member of VAM will show up to try and avenge Tuck's death. Just sit down!" She forcefully pointed to a leather recliner we had placed in the corner. I respected her wishes but only because she was my grandmother.

The cleanup crew appeared in minutes, removing only one corpse from the bunker, telling me Jon was still alive. I wondered if Shelton already knew what happened here today.

The cleaning guys loaded up their white work van, shook hands with the now human, Cam and Rayan and departed with their load. Cam and Rayan quickly disappeared back into the bunker.

I was anxious for Cam to make his way back to me, my stomach queasy with butterflies, unsure if it was hunger pains or something else. I placed my hand over my belly and took a deep breath.

"Grandmother, do you ever wish you could have had children by Rayan?" I said.

"That was random, Marry." She turned to face me. A little taken back by the question but she answered it anyways. "Honey, Rayan, and I were always enough for one another. We loved spending time alone, together. We had your father to look after, and I always felt like Rayan viewed Cam as a son. Both of our plates were full." She said.

Her answer was honest, and I appreciated that.

"Do you have any regrets?" I said.

"I fear that when I approach my human death at a terribly old age, I will regret knowing that the love of my life will remain here without me. I haven't any regrets thus far but that could be the one thing I wish I'd done differently when the time comes." She said. Grandmother leaned her head back and groaned, miserably thinking about what the future was destined to hold.

Her words caused my heart to ache.

"So, have Rayan change you, become immortal. We don't have to leave our husbands at any time. The whole idea just scares me." I said. I knew it wasn't something she'd ever do, and she understood the same about me.

"Against my beliefs, Marry! Against my beliefs." She said twice so I didn't miss the point.

The same reason my mother never agreed to the change and the reason I upheld her wishes when Cam offered to change her around the time of her death.

Deep in thought, I caught a glimpse of someone walking up the hill from the bunker. I got up, went to the window and squinted to get a good look. "Jon." I whispered.

There was no sign of Cam or Rayan. A sudden urge to run down to the barn came over me. As soon as I began to dart in that direction, someone gently grabbed me from behind. I slowly turned around to find Cam holding me. Rayan stood a few feet behind Cam.

Both laughed, Rayan spoke up. "So, you ladies want to be turned into vampires? Is that what we overheard?" Both allowed their fangs to emerge, letting out a subtle hiss.

Cam moved in towards my upper body, mouth wide and with an evil grin. "There is nothing I would love to do more than change you, Mrs. Rosenthal… into a vampire." Cam said.

Rayan took a quick nibble from grandmother's neck causing a small drop of blood to emerge.

Grandmother smacked him and then placed her hand over her mouth in shock that he had done such a thing. We all laughed at her facial expression.

Laughter and love, I believed that to be our family motto.

"Fun and games aside, where is Jon going as if nothing happened?" I said. No one responded. "Hello!" I snapped. "Did you hear my question? Jon is just walking away! Why?" I said.

"Calm down, Marry! Isn't that what you wanted?" Cam said.

"No! So, that's it, you just let him go free?" I said, throwing my hands up out of frustration.

"Trust me sweetie, he's not going to do anything stupid. He had front row seats to everything that unfolded here today. He doesn't want to relive any of it and especially not as the victim." Cam had a way with words. "He's tuning back into his regularly scheduled life. He'll be going back to work and hopefully soon he will start his own family." Cam laughed.

"He would actually make a wonderful father.... now." Rayan chimed in.

"One thing is certain; he will never break any kind of law again whether it's human trafficking or speeding in his vehicle." Cam said causing the brothers to double over in laughter.

"What about Tuck?" I asked. "Do you believe Shelton and his group will respond to his death?" I said.

"During Shelton's hospital visit with Wesley, he gave him the go ahead to proceed how he wished where Tuck was concerned and that Tuck was a liability to VAM but worse than that, he was a disgrace. Killing him was a favor to Shelton." Cam said.

It was sad but no worse than what Stevie was put through.

"Stevie." I wondered aloud how he was doing on the farm.

"I've kept up with him from a distance. He is doing

excellent and has a surprise for us, Marry." Cam said.

What on earth could Stevie possibly have for the two of us. I hoped the frown on my face wasn't evident.

"Shall we pay him a visit tomorrow, my love?" Cam said.

I rolled my eyes towards the ceiling, not sure that I was willing to accept a gift from Stevie.

Rayan interrupted the conversation before my disrespect was addressed. "Ah, I'm overheated and in need of some rest." He fanned himself with a magazine from the table.

Cam agreed, leaned down, and pecked my cheek with his cold, red lips before exiting the room. I struggled to give him a smile, wiping his kiss away with the back of my hand.

My grandmother and I took a seat in the matching rocking chairs, placed side by side on the patio. I enjoyed quality time alone with her and the conversations we had. I thought about sharing our plan to become parents but was worried about her reaction.

"Marry, what's going on with you, dear?" Grandmother asked. "You have had quite the attitude with your husband. I fear he will at some point respond to your ill nature."

I gently rocked back and forth while the late afternoon wind blew through my hair. I leaned my head back and sighed. "Grandmother." I said.

She turned to look at me.

"I'm thankful I have you and for all the things you did to protect me and my mother." I said. I could feel the tears welling up in my eyes.

She kept her composure though her deep, quivering inhalation gave a clue to her emotions. "Marry, I doubt you would have gone without, you or your mother. Cam has always been two steps ahead of you whether you knew it or not." She said.

"That doesn't minimize everything you did for us. I love you very much and wouldn't trade the time I have had with you for the world." I said.

"God willing, I will be around for many, many, many more years!" She said.

"Back to my original question. What's been going on with you?" She said.

I hesitated for a brief moment.

"Well?" She said.

I hung my head and mumbled. "Cam and I are trying to have a baby. He has doctors on his payroll that proclaim to have mastered this conception thing so that our baby would not be cursed with any Vampire DNA." I said.

"Repeat that and speak up!" She said.

This time, I held my head high, unashamed of our decision to try and conceive. I told her exactly what we had done.

"Do you trust that? Do you think it's possible to remove Cam's Vampire DNA from his seed? Don't get me wrong - I would absolutely love for the two of you to have cute little human babies! I would love a great grandchild! I guess what I'm asking is how do you really feel about this?" She said.

I paused my rocking, folded my hands, and looked her directly in the eye.

"I didn't want a baby. But Cam's desire for a child is overwhelming. I love him enough to try. The procedure was performed two days ago when we were in Memphis. The doctor felt like our chances of becoming pregnant were pretty good. We will go back next week to see." I spoke fast hoping to curve her reaction.

She raised her eyebrows and blinked quickly. "Well, my dear, if this is what you and Cam want then I support you one hundred percent. I think you will make an excellent mother." She said.

"Thank you." I replied.

We sat rocking in silence until the sun went down.

CHAPTER 15

I scarfed down a turkey wrap, even eyeballed grandmother's leftovers but chose not to sink low enough to ask her for them. I wished her a good night and made my way down the hall. The biggest belch I had ever created in my entire life snuck out and echoed through the room.

"Marry. "Grandmother said.

I placed my hand over my mouth and looked towards Cherry who was in the kitchen, snickering. "I am so sorry." I said trying to hold in my giggle.

I decided to check in on Skylar before heading up to join Cam for a good night's rest. I pulled his door open slightly enough to peek in. Skylar didn't miss a beat.

"Hey Marry, come in here." He said, still wide awake. I think the excitement of the new room and being out of the dreary hospital wouldn't let him sleep.

"What are you doing?" I said.

"I'm trying to play this game. See, look over there. You have to steer the car down the road and avoid hitting things." He said. He shook his hands. "My hands feel funny, tingly and I can't move them the way I want to."

I sat down in the gaming chair next to his bed. I placed my hands on top of his and gave them a good rub. I knew his body was finally beginning to wake up from the years of non-movement. I picked up the controller and showed him how the game was meant to be played, moving from side to side in the chair, screaming at every near miss of the items in my way. It wasn't too long before I could hear Skylar's breathing become heavy, He had dozed off. I guess that was enough fun for one night.

I gently placed the controller on his nightstand and tiptoed my way to the door, just as I was about to open it, Skylar whispered that he loved me. I placed my hand up to my lips, kissing it and then waving it back towards Skylar.

"Mwah! I love you too, buddy, good night." I told him.

"What took you so long?" Cam raised his head from the pillow as soon as I made entry to our quarters. A small light flickered in the corner allowing me to see him in the dark, his face nearly glowing, his eyelids small, open enough just to see me.

I told him of my adventures with Skylar and how he had fallen fast asleep while I pretended to drive a race car. He pulled the sheets back, motioning for me to come to bed. I slid in with him and embraced his tender touch. My sleep, finally peaceful.

"Cam, get up." I said. I ran over, hopped on the bed, and began to jump. "It's a beautiful day for the plans we have." I told him. The sun made its way through the corner of the curtain, I could hear the wind hit against the window.

"Be careful." He said, reaching for my arm. I allowed him to pick me up and place me back on the floor.

"You are so strong." I said, then laughed.

"Mhmm, you haven't seen anything yet." He said.

Suddenly, he froze. His eyes quickly scanned the room, he inhaled the air, turning his nose up to something he perceived as foul.

"Wait right here, I'll be back." He said, flying down the steps.

I waited patiently, watching the second hand make its rounds until nearly fifteen minutes had passed. An uneasy feeling came over me. I had to go check on Cam. I couldn't stop myself. I made it to the bottom floor; the place was empty and terrifyingly quiet. My vision blurred, I closed my eyes in an attempt to correct it, reopening them only to find my mother sitting on our patio swing, holding the same baby boy I had once before witnessed with her. I walked closer to the back door.

This time was very different, Maggie was with her. Maggie's golden hair held a pink flower. She was perfect, with no flaws or signs of abuse. She twirled around, holding a baby girl high above her head and bringing her down only to place a kiss on the child's forehead. Both babies giggled as mother and Maggie cheerfully sang Mary had a little lamb.

I was weak from sadness, missing them so much. I turned my head away from the scene, taking three deep breaths, I looked back. They were gone. I supposed hallucinations came with the anxiety I felt most days.

I called out for Cam, no response. I heard a whisper coming from the staff's living area.

"Your stay here was over yesterday, you being here is a violation of EVG ethics." Cam said, unaware that I was now right behind him as he stood at the door to what was once Sasha's room.

"I forgot something." Sasha said leaning over adding clothing to her bag. Her blouse revealing that which should have been kept hidden. She looked up at me with an evil grin. "You're lucky I no longer have a place here, human."

Cam quickly spun around, hissing, bringing attention to his fangs.

"I would've had your man in no time." Sasha said.

Cam abruptly entered the room, slammed the door, and exited within a matter of seconds. The gentlemen in the white van arrived in minutes to take away the jezebel of a corpse.

"Never doubt my faithfulness to you, Marry. You are my true love, for always." Cam said. He put his arm around me and summoned Juan to bring my car around to the front.

"Let's check on Skylar before we leave, shall we?" Cam said.

"As long as he doesn't try and convince me to give up the day's activities to play video games because I just might do it!" I joked.

We both went unbothered by the unlucky turn of events for Sasha.

Cam swung Skylar's door open, startling the child.

"Hey, buddy, we're headed out for a while. You don't need anything do you?" Cam asked.

Skylar's face lit up. He waved his hands throughout the room. "I have everything!"

"See you soon, then." Cam added.

"Have fun and I love you." Skylar said.

"Ahhhh.. He told me he loved me yesterday, too." I said as we walked through the foyer on our way out the door.

"He does love you Marry; he can see how real your kindness is by looking in your eyes, not everyone has that sense, you know? Children can tell and animals of the sort, they know, too." He laughed referring to himself. Cam doesn't realize just how much of an animal he is…... Not!

He opened the passenger side door for me as he had always done. I thought back to my first day of school in Rhode Island when he gifted me the car. He drove me there, maneuvering at such a high rate of speed that I joyously screamed, pleasured by the thrill of living on the edge, unaware it would become my forever.

I wiped away the tears that began to form. I didn't want Cam to see my sadness. After the conversation grandmother and I had the other night, I suspected forever, always was an option for me. The thought of being without Cam hurt me that much! I loved him with everything in me.

"What are you thinking about?" Cam said.

I smiled. "You! I'm thinking about you, always."

"As you should!" Cam's happiness was a bright shining light today. He gleamed with such brilliance.

In no time we were whipping into the driveway of the old farmhouse. I squinted my eyes to be sure we were at our destination; our arrival was strangely fast.

The car kicked up gravel, hitting the undercarriage loudly, piercing my ears. Tiny dust tornadoes flew around dirtying my black Benz.

"Cam, you will have to wash my car for me now and I mean it." I said. I hated a nasty car.

"Maybe you could have Stevie clean it up before we head back home. I don't feel comfortable riding in such filth."

"Mmmmm." Cam raised his eyebrows.

When we pulled around to the back of the house, Stevie was outside feeding the chickens.

"Did we have chickens before, Cam?" I said.

I was shocked to see the little animals, but they were comical and pleasant. The way they strutted around like they owned the place made me laugh.

"No, we didn't but whatever it takes to keep Stevie clean and happy, I suppose. He seems to like those chickens and he bought them himself which is a major improvement. Spending his money on Farm animals and not dope - I'll take that any day." He said.

Stevie turned around when he heard our car doors shut. "Hey Cam, Mrs. Marry." He tilted his baseball cap to great us. At that moment I wouldn't have been surprised if he had a piece of hay hanging from his mouth, chewing on it. I was disappointed to find he didn't.

He looked better. He was no longer shaking, well-groomed and polite as ever.

"I see you got you some chickens there, Stevie?" Cam said.

"Yes Sir, I like those little fellas. They give me something to take care of while I'm getting myself together." He smiled and continued.

"Shelton stopped by here earlier, He said he appreciates what you're doing for me. He even allowed me to schedule a feeding. I go tomorrow for the first time in I don't know how long. I've not made it back into the group but I'm heading in the right direction." Stevie peered at the ground and kicked through a group of grass blades.

"That's great news Buddy." I knew Cam was genuinely happy for him as was I.

"I owe you, Cam. I know I'm going to succeed this time,

not a doubt the one. All I needed was someone to believe in me."

I began to cry, moved by his admission.

"Mrs. Marry, please don't cry. I didn't mean to upset you. I guess women in the family way have a bit of a hard time controlling their emotions." Stevie glanced back up but only for a split second.

Cam and I traded looks.

"I have a little something for both of you and I really hope you like it. It's been a hobby of mine for some time now. I just haven't done it in years seeing as my mind was pretty messed up." Stevie started walking towards the house, we followed.

"What on earth could it be?" I spoke my thoughts out loud. Cam turned to look at me, squinching his eyebrows, I raised mine in response to him.

A light fixture now hung in the living room that once only had candles.

"I took my last paycheck and had the electric and water turned on in my name. I figured that's the least I could do seeing as you're letting me stay here rent free and all." Stevie continued into the hallway, flipping the switch to illuminate the area.

Cam nodded, pleased with Stevie's progression.

Stevie blushed and a slight smile formed on his face knowing he had made Cam proud. Stevie stepped back out of our way and pointed into the furthest bedroom. "It's in there, go take a look." He said.

Cam cut his eyes, moved in front of me and slowly stepped around the corner and then into the room. A large bloody tear began to run down his face. "Marry." Cam whispered.

Confused by Cam's sudden behavior change, I hurriedly moved by his side. In the middle of the room sat the most beautiful hand-made solid oak cradle I had ever seen in my life. Its magnificence took my breath away.

"It's for your baby." Stevie rubbed his hand across the smooth slats. "I don't know how I know about that child coming, I just do. It'll be a blessing for you both. Y'all do so much good for others, God is rewarding you, I believe that." Stevie said.

Cam and I stood in a daze, feeling like my pregnancy had been confirmed a hundred times over, just not by the actual doctor.

"So, you say you just have a feeling that my wife here is with child, Stevie?" Cam asked.

"I have these dreams, they're right vivid, Marry's always in the background, kind of hovering there, watching. I see another woman dancing around carrying a little baby boy in her arms, sometimes rocking him a chair. I intend to make you a rocker just like it, too." Stevie grinned as if everything he said was fact and then shyly looked back towards the floor. I believed what he was saying, having had similar dreams and visions of my own.

"Ah, I see." Cam tried to keep a straight face. "You've been dreaming about my wife, have you?"

Stevie's eyes widened; he began to stutter. "No sir, Cam. No sir, not all."

"Calm down. It was a joke." Cam laughed.

"Hey, Cam." Stevie spoke quietly. "I want to thank y'all for what you're doing for my nephew, Skylar. Shelton told me that too, but I'm supposed to be quiet about it or my chances of reentry to VAM will be terminated. He said it was a favor to Wesley." He looked Cam directly in the eyes for less than a second.

Cam didn't have anything to say regarding Skylar.

Cam reached for his wallet almost unable to pull it from his pant pocket. He had gained weight, and I hadn't noticed it until now. "How much do I owe you for that awesomely made baby bed, son?" Cam asked Stevie.

"Nawl, now Cam, I said that's a gift. Let me finally do something nice for somebody – Please now, means a lot to me." Stevie's solemn expression was heartbreaking.

"I'll send Rayan back with the truck to get it. There's no way it's going to fit in that little Benz out there." Cam reached out and shook Stevie's hand. "Much obliged, partner."

"Yes sir, we really appreciate it." I added. "That's the finest piece of craftmanship I've ever seen."

"We'll see ya." Stevie said as we got in the car and waved bye to him.

"I love you, Marry." Cam said as we turned onto the main road heading into town. I smiled, looked towards him and positioned my mouth to repeat his words back to him. The rearview mirror caught my attention before I could speak.

"The police are following us, and they have their blue lights on." I panicked, breathing heavily, placing my hand over my stomach to try and calm the butterflies.

"We haven't done anything wrong and if we are guilty of something, it would be irrelevant." He laughed realizing my human mind was overrunning with fear.

The wind had begun to blow, the sun disappeared under dark clouds as tiny sprinkles of rain landed on the windshield.

"Aren't you going to pull over?" I asked him.

"No!" He answered just as the vehicle sped around us. "Well, looka there. They gave Jon another squad car."

Jon was driving the vehicle. He blew his horn and waved at us. Cam gestured back.

"I suppose it's safe to say, he harbors no ill feelings towards us." I joked.

"None at all." We both laughed.

He took my hand and placed it on his thigh. He gently squeezed it, the cold from his palm sent chills through my body.

"I've always wanted a family of my own, one that I could love and cherish and provide for. I will be the man my father was not, a promise unbreakable to you, Marry."

CHAPTER 16

"If we miss our flight, I will have to carry us there and you remember how sick that made you last time." Cam was a bit fussy this morning.

I was moving slowly and had been for nearly a week. We were flying to Memphis with Dr. Patak to confirm my pregnancy. He couldn't be a hundred percent sure here at the house, so he recommended we travel back to his office where we would have access to state-of-the-art equipment.

I moped across the floor, dragging my feet.

"Just come here." Cam pulled me gently by the arm, lifting me and carrying me to the car.

Dr. Patak followed.

Juan dropped us off at the airport and we boarded our flight soon after.

Neither of us spoke to Dr. Patak all the way to Tennessee. I didn't have the energy and Cam sat with his face planted in a newspaper. It was his way of avoiding conversation. Cam had always distanced himself from his workers when it came to personal matters. I knew what was going on in that thick skull of his, we would only discuss our child in an office setting. I agreed with that. After all there was someone flying this plane and Cam trusted very few.

Once we landed, a member of EVG picked the three of us up and drove us to the hospital. The drive there was just as silent as the plane trip. I leaned my head on the window, the tint preventing anyone outside from looking in. I began to daydream about what was to come. I was excited but also scared.

I felt his ice-cold fingertips touch my arm. "Sit up, darling, we've arrived." Cam spoke softly.

I yawned loudly to which he raised his brows.

Dr. Patak was already outside of the vehicle.

"We will enter through the back as usual." Cam directed

him.

Dr. Patak escorted us to a patient room. "Wait here." He said.

The door shut loudly causing me to cover my ears. Cam sat in a corner chair with his legs crossed, once again reading the paper. He didn't notice my discomfort.

"Are we ready to find out?" Dr. Patak backed through the door pulling a cart that held an ultrasound machine. His white coat was the only thing I could focus on.

"We could have done this at home if all you needed was an ultrasound." I snipped.

Cam shook his paper, lowered it, and then uncrossed his legs. "Why the bad attitude, my dear Marry?" He chuckled and then under his breath whispered something along the lines of liking it when I acted that way.

"Oh no, Mrs. Marry, it's much more vigilant and has the capabilities to detect what we're looking for, something a little bit different than most normal pregnancies." Dr. Patak slid the contraption closer to me.

He pricked my finger with a tiny needle, put my blood immediately on a slide and then under a microscope. He sat down on a stool placed in front of the cabinet, reached into a drawer, and handed me a hospital gown, all the while studying the specimen. Never looking away, he reached behind him and handed me the gown. Put this on and lay on the bed, please." He instructed.

"Alrighy." Dr. Patak said as he stood up and made his way over to me, returning to his original position only to retrieve a pair of latex gloves. He covered me with a paper sheet and had me lay further back. He then exposed my stomach. "This will be slightly cold." He said as he squirted a blue gel on my belly.

"Cam, please hit the light switch." The machine began to buzz once turned on. The dark room and the cold caused me to yawn. I was ready for a nap at any given moment.

He gently maneuvered the device over my stomach, at

times pressing a little harder. He stared at the screen as did I, unsure of what I was seeing.

"Cam, come closer." Dr. Patak replaced his own hand with Cam's. "Hold it steady and now look at the monitor. Marry, that's your baby!" Dr. Patak wiped his eyes, about to cry himself.

"He or she is no bigger than a green pea."

Cam grabbed my hand and squeezed hard. "Thank you, doctor!" Cam said. "Thank you!"

His dream was now becoming a reality. We were going to be a real family after all.

Dr. Patak gave me a strict diet to follow. I didn't need the fruits and veggies most future mothers required, it was red meat for me and a lot of it. He also insisted that I keep my stress to a minimum.

I looked Cam square in his eyes. "He controls that, sir." I told Dr. Patak.

The instructions he had for Cam were going to be a lot harder. "Cam, Keep her happy!"

"Yeah Cam, keep me happy." I giggled.

"Don't I always?" He asked. I crossed my eyes at him and sighed.

"Well momma, I will do my absolute best." Cam brought my hand up to his lips and ever so softly kissed over each of my fingers.

We thanked Dr. Patak and began to head out of the room having already made plans for the two of us to fly back to Charlotte, alone.

I tugged at Cam's arm, pulling him down to my level and whispered in his ear. "Don't you have something for the doctor? You normally leave him an envelope."

His smile faded. "Marry, trust me when I say he does not need anything extra. He is staying at our home and caring for Skylar and will now be tasked with keeping an extra eye on you, my dear. If you only knew what that man is making - you would insist I make him leave." He laughed.

He wrapped his arms around my waist in an attempt to carry me out of the hospital.

"No, Cam. I can walk." I smacked his hand.

He shrugged, taking my hand instead. My stomach let out a hideous growl. Cam stopped in his tracks and looked at me with confusion.

"Ah, I know just the place. First, stop, Sully's steak house on Third Avenue and Taylor Street." He promised me the best steak in Memphis.

I could barely wait to arrive, uncomfortable from the rumblings.

I cut into my steak, medium rare was the taste I acquired, leaned over my plate, and took a huge bite almost unable to chew. My cheeks poked out and a bit of juice dripped down my chin.

Cam silently stared in my direction.

"What"? I said with a mouthful of Prime Rib.

"Nothing, my dear. I'm glad to see you're enjoying your meal." He nonchalantly called for our waitress with a quick flick of the wrist. "Si, please, miss." He spoke to her. A tall, thin, young man returned to the table carrying a red leather menu, the pages outlined in gold.

"Mr. Rosenthal, pleasure to see you. What can I do for you this evening?" The waiter asked.

"Give me just a moment please, Si."

"You know him?" I asked.

"I do." He answered me quickly and offered no explanation. Cam motioned for Si to return to the table. "I'll have a glass of your finest Vampagne." He folded the menu shut and handed it back to Si.

The room had a dark atmosphere, the lights turned down low, the subtle hint of whispering between couples and the occasional dinging noise from glasses and silverware. I wasn't comfortable here, but my peace wasn't disturbed either.

A gold chalice full of a thick red substance was placed in front of Cam. When I glanced up, the waiter had disappeared. I scanned the room to see how many of the other patrons were drinking the same as him.

"Sharon is here and she's not with Ken. Nope, that's definitely not her husband." I said. "Let's go, please." I wanted to avoid a confrontation.

Cam pretended not to be concerned, he retrieved our check and paid the bill. He intertwined his arm with mine and we walked out.

The driver pulled up as soon as we made our exit, Cam opened the door for me, and I slid across the backseat. I turned my focus to the window and gazed out amongst the many skyscrapers that covered the night sky trying to avoid eye contact with Cam.

"Look at me." Cam said. I slowly turned my head towards him. "What is it? Spill it! What are you holding in?"

I waited for the car to slowly pull off before I spoke. "The man Sharon was with…" I paused.

"…Was Shelton." I spoke calmly hoping he wouldn't react.

Cam pounded the headrest on the driver's seat. "Back to the restaurant immediately!" He yelled.

The car made a U-turn, nearly hitting a pedestrian. We sped back in the direction of the steak house.

"Slow down!" I cried. "Cam, make him slow down! Nothing should be more important than me and this…." I stopped myself before saying baby.

Perfect timing, Sharon and Shelton were hugging on their way out and just as they were about to lock lips, Cam jumped out of the car.

"Shelton!" I could hear Cam call his name through the now closed car door.

"Hello, Cam." I watched as Shelton reached his hand out to shake Cam's. Cam refused his gesture.

"Sharon, what are you doing with Shelton? You can't

even take care of your own child and seemingly not your own husband else he would be here with you." Cam's approach always lacked tactic and rarely did he stop and think before acting.

"Shelton, do you care to answer since your mistress does not?" Cam took a step closer to Shelton, his voice became louder.

Sharon looked towards the ground and snickered. I wanted to get out and beat her myself but that wasn't an option for me, for a few reasons.

I could tell Shelton was uneasy with the situation, he took a step back, away from Cam, not because he was frightened of him, but Shelton had a reputation to uphold. He was a much older vampire and had conditioned himself to be the likes of a corporate executive and in a way, that's much of what he was, just with extreme powers.

Cam wasn't scared of Shelton either, but he was more of a fly by the seat of your pants type vampire. He was ready for anything whether he started it or not.

Cam took another step closer to Shelton and this time Shelton felt the disrespect. It was obvious when he returned the movement and went in towards Cam. I couldn't believe this was happening. The tips of their noses were nearly touching from their closeness.

Swirling leaves bounced from the street as mother nature reared her head. The skies became darker, thunder clapped. I could see the anger growing in Shelton's face and neither of them were willing to retreat or so I thought.

Shelton finally spoke "Cam, let the two of us go sit in your car for a moment." He waved his hand toward Sharon causing her to disappear in the night. "She's no love of mine, we have a business agreement for which I owe no one an explanation. Especially, the likes of you, Cameron. However, it may be cute to converse with you." Shelton's face became stone cold, bringing out his pointy nose and ears, his features were thin and bony though his stature was grand.

"Watch how you speak to me in my territory." Cam said as he opened the car door. I couldn't believe he was allowing the leader of VAM into a vehicle with me and his unborn child.

"Cameron, I am trying to work with you here. I have been more than kind to you and your people. But I cannot and will not tolerate this nonsense." Shelton removed the one leg he had already placed into the car. "I'm not doing this with you, son. You can handle this how you see fit unless you have something to offer me, my dear boy."

I could feel my face flush with heat, Shelton's voice was nearly debilitating. I nervously shook in my seat.

Shelton put pressure on the tip of his cane and then leaned down to see me, tipping his hat signifying he was about to make his exit. He then quickly made his way to the other side of the street.

Cam followed behind him, his trench coat blew in the wind. Cam yelled out to Shelton. "Is your information worth my money?" He asked.

"I would say so." Shelton said, chuckling. "And especially if you want to rid that jezebel from your group and keep her from sniffing out the boy. She's on his tracks, you know."

Cam didn't always conduct himself in the best manner, but he had no problem with buying whatever he wanted. We both knew Shelton didn't need Cam's money, but any currency placed into VAM's pocket by a member of EVG was a win for VAM and vice-versa. The information could've been free, but Cam's temper got in the way.

Cam opened the car door once again but before Shelton could get it, I jumped out. "Excuse me, Shelton. I need to speak to my husband for just a moment, please." I said.

Shelton grinned allowing only one fang to distend. "Sorry, miss. Old habits do die hard." He shot a glance towards Cam who pretended not to see what just transpired.

I knew the look in Cam's eyes all too well. He wasn't concerned with Shelton's threatening mannerisms because he intended to get the information he wanted and then kill Shelton.

"Cam, can you please escort me to the restroom? I can't hold it." I grabbed his hand.

He released himself from my grip and stuck his head back into the car to tell Shelton we would return momentarily.

We walked hand in hand through the glass doors and to the back of the restaurant where the bathrooms were located. I pulled him in close enough to me where I could whisper into his ear. "I have been with you and married to you for quite some while. I know your facial expressions like my own and I know exactly what state of mind you are in right now. Whatever it is you are thinking, I am begging you as your wife, not to act on those thoughts. I know you feel disrespected, and the time will come when you can address that. But not now, for the sake of me and this child."

Cam made awkward movements with his mouth, squinting his eyes, and breathing deeply. "What? I wasn't going to do anything." His voice squealed as he tried to convince me.

"We need him around for more reasons than you can see. You're being blinded by your anger. I love you, Cam!" Tears began to well in my eyes.

He leaned his arm over my head and pushed the door open, nudging me into the ladies' room. His fangs evolved, hissing into the air, he sent every woman around scurrying out like little mice. He began to kiss me. In his rage full of passion, he drank of my blood, sparingly, but enough to satisfy his urge.

We exited as if nothing happened, and the people around dared not say a word.

"I love you, my sweet Marry." He spoke gently.

I loved him too, choosing not to say the words, I smiled.

Shelton surprisingly waited for our return. Cam opened the car door for me, and I got in. Shelton followed and then Cam quickly shut the door behind him.

"Driver, drive." He instructed. We drove around and around the city while Cam and Shelton conversed. Cam's attitude had changed drastically and for the better.

"Why were you with Sharon tonight?" Cam wasted no time to begin the questioning.

"She called me here, I obliged her out of curiosity, wondering why one such as herself would summon I, seeing as our business was and is handled by my associates." Shelton said.

Cam never took his eyes off Shelton.

"She wanted to talk to me about her son, Skylar. I ignored her plea, unsure of the motive. Her actions then became seductive in manner as if to try and sway me with her beauty but anyone that knows me knows that I do not participate in any activities outside of my marriage to Betsy. I can only be tempted by the root of all evil." He laughed. "Cam, you understand, don't you?" He asked.

"Shelton, in all honesty and please do not take offense to this, temptation has never become me, I act only on my true feelings. There are only some moments, if my wife is persuasive enough that I may possibly give in to her." Cam smiled, sending me a subliminal message.

"Hmmm." Shelton folded his hands.

"What happened after that?" Cam said.

"She tried to convince me that Skylar was half VAM, and that Wesley was in on to her secret. She hadn't a clue that I was aware she tried to kill Skylar, herself. I also know that a child of that magnitude could not exist. It's biologically impossible." Shelton continued speaking as Cam and I focused strictly on him.

"She believes that Wesley had Skylar moved from the hospital to an undisclosed location. She also believes the trip he is sending her on to Europe is bogus, so she purposely missed her flight. She intends to finish the job she began, that act of killing her child."

What Shelton was saying made sense but there was still one thing bothering me. Cam asked Shelton exactly what I was thinking. "What does any of this have to do with you?"

Shelton chuckled. "In her own words, she heard I would do favors for others if the price was right, too bad what she offered me was chump change, that was until she tried to throw in some of Wesley's money as if she had access to it. Don't get me wrong Cam." Shelton sighed. "As intriguing as those numbers were, I'm no fool."

"She wanted you to pretend to be Skylar's father so she could gain access to him through you, hoping that you could persuade Wesley to disclose his where abouts?" Cam said.

"Mmmm…. Aren't you one smart cookie." Shelton's abnormally deep laugh caused Cam to hiss in his direction.

"I'm nobody's cookie, old man! Care to find out?" Cam quipped.

"Calm down, son. It was a joke, but you too should rest assured that I am no one's old man." Shelton said. "None of her requests made any sense to me. I couldn't play the part of that boy's father. I was soon to bid her farewell once we exited the establishment, that was until you stopped us. She's a very crooked individual."

I believed Shelton knew Skylar was half VAM but this whole time he maintained the idea as ludicrous.

"Driver, take the gentleman back to our original spot." Cam said.

Cam pulled one of his infamous envelopes from his coat pocket and handed it to Shelton. The car came to an abrupt stop, the two shook hands and Shelton went on his way.

"Was that bit of information worth the money?" I asked Cam. "And do you believe he doesn't know Skylar is half VAM?"

"Shelton doesn't know Skylar is half VAM. Neither Welsey nor I have ever mentioned Skylar's breed to him. But I do view this all very strangely. Sharon felt comfortable approaching Shelton with her problem and that is odd. I'm no fool, my dear." Cam said. "No fool at all."

"It'll come to light." I whispered, thinking aloud.

"Oh, and to answer your other question, the information was well worth my money. Someone will suffer behind Shelton's greediness." Cam said.

It was getting late. I yawned and then added another yawn at the end of my first one, it was fake. I hoped Cam would speed up the process of whatever it was we were now doing so I could get home.

"You want to go stay at the Peabody? It's right around the corner." He laughed knowing my new fear of its haunted ambiance.

"No! Another place maybe but not there." I slapped his leg.

"Nothing else around here is worth my money. Driver, take us to the airport." Cam said.

We boarded our plane immediately after arrival.

"Rest now, my love." He kissed me gently on the lips, his love was like a sedative. I fell fast asleep.

CHAPTER 17

T.F. Green Airport - Rhode Island. The sign was the only thing I could see coming in for a landing. "Why are we here?" I asked. I expected to arrive back home in North Carolina.

"I think often of the time we spent together when you were younger. My soul has always longed for you, drawn me to you. My desire is to relive some of those moments before our child is born, remind you what you mean to me. Therefore, I hope you will join me in the bunker on your grandmother's property for a couple of nights filled with marital bliss, just the two of us." Cam said.

He smiled; a small portion of fang caught my attention. I was a sucker for romance.

"There's nothing I would love more." I could remember every second of every minute spent with Cam, the good, the bad, the ugly and the beautiful, all of it combined formed the most passionate love one could experience.

"Where is Read?" I asked. He had occupied the barn for so long, I was a little worried the three of us would be staying together.

Cam broke out into a fit of laughter. "Read is dating a set of twins and they're all staying together under one roof in Warwick. It won't last long. The old boy has really stepped out of character with this one."

"Oh. I wonder how many stories Read's twins have heard by now?" I laughed right along with Cam.

A newer model white Jaguar whipped up beside us. The driver stepped out moving almost as quickly as he drove. "Hop in. Let me get you to where you need to go." He said.

I loved the staff that wasted no time getting their jobs done.

Once inside, I took a deep breath, inhaling the aroma. "What on earth are you doing?" Cam said.

"It smells so good in here. The newness is inviting. I

really like this car." I was shocked that the smell didn't sicken me like most everything else.

"Do you wish for a car such as this?" Cam said.

"Maybe." I left room for a change of mind, there might be something I liked better.

"It would be most stunning with a car seat buckled in the back." He smiled.

It was close to midnight when we rounded the corner into grandmother and Rayan's neighborhood. A shadowy figure emerged from the house where Sarah once lived with her human family. Also, the place where Wesley saved her from the terminal illness she had been plagued with as a child. Her family couldn't afford proper medical treatment to sustain her life. Wesley's visits to the Children's hospital allowed him to already have a relationship with her. Wesley hadn't a choice but to do what he did. He knew the pain her mother and grandfather suffered after he took her, but he loved her enough to inflict it upon them. Her biological father left once he realized he could no longer support the family. The grandfather moved in to try and help but on his fixed income it was impossible.

I nudged Cam to get his attention. "Cam, what's going on at Sarah's grandfather's house?" He quickly turned to look. "That is Sarah, Marry! And Benji! Stop the car!" He yelled at the driver.

"Wait here, Marry." Cam said.

"I'm not." I got out of the car just as fast as he did.

"Get in the car." He whispered through clenched teeth to Sarah who blatantly refused.

"I want to see my family." Sarah red faced and teary eyed shouted at Cam.

"They are not your family. Get in the car." Cam's stern approach did no good.

Benji shrugged his shoulders and pleaded with her in a last-ditch effort.

"Why does she think these people are her family?" Cam

asked, while walking towards her. Without waiting for a reply, he grabbed her, flew her in the car and pinned her down, leaving me and Benji to walk the rest of the way to grandmothers. The car swayed from left to right all the way up the hill. I imagined she was still trying to wrestle with him to let her go.

"Why is she doing this Benji?" I asked.

"About a week ago Sharon told her some lame story about Wesley stealing her from a good and loving family and how her life would have been perfect had she not been kidnapped. Sarah held it in and tried to ignore her, but it was as if Sharon kept taunting her with this, saying little things to get her worked up. Then tonight she couldn't take it anymore. She wanted to see for herself. I followed her here." Benji's bottom lip began to quiver.

"Marry, that house is empty." Benji hung his head, hurting for Sarah.

Sarah had always known what occurred between her and Wesley and that he saved her life, but Sharon was trying to make her believe she was kidnapped instead of healed of her sickness and blessed with a new family.

The walk was a bit much for me. It was dark and every branch in the trees around us crackled at the slightest breeze, luckily Cam sent the driver back down to get us.

Cam had managed to calm Sarah by the time we entered the house. I sat down next to her and rubbed her pretty hair away from her face. "Sarah." I said. "There's no one in that house and you know that I would never lie to you. I love you! Wesley didn't kidnap you. He loves you more than I do and that's a lot of love."

Sarah halfway smiled.

"Cam will handle this, right Cam?" I looked at him through the corner of my eyes.

"Oh yes, yes I will. I will handle this, consider it handled." Cam began fidgeting with his fingers. I had never witnessed him do that before. I believed he had gone mad, reaching a new level of anger.

"Do y'all want to play that game my mother used to love? Win, lose or draw? Cam, Benji, don't you remember the fun times? Sarah here hasn't got to play with us, and I think she would really enjoy it!" Benji and Cam began to laugh, and the thought of our game nights did me some good, too. Sarah agreed. I took her by the hand and led her to the dining room. Cam and Benji lagged behind.

"In the morning, you take her back to Denver, you keep her away from Sharon and you do whatever it takes to make her the happiest female on this planet. Do you understand?" Cam sternly spoke to Benji. I was accustomed to listening to conversations I shouldn't hear.

"That's always been my goal, to make her happy, Cam. I have no problem with what you're asking me to do." Benji was such a sweetheart.

Cam patted Benji on the back as they entered the room. I knew in my heart; he would one day make Sarah a fine husband. Sharon would pay for her sins toward Sarah quicker than she would the crimes against her own son. She had to know what was coming. I felt like Sharon was inviting all this trouble.

CHAPTER 18

"Sarah's gone! Cam, Sarah's gone!" Benjamin frantically ran through our bedroom door, shaking Cam to wake him.

"Don't do that! He doesn't do well when startled." I said to Benji.

"Cam, baby, wake up. Benji says Sarah is missing." I gently rubbed his forehead as he lay next to me in our king size bed, his arms crossed at the waist in front of him. The top half of his body sprung up, he sat there dazed for a split second, realizing Benji was standing next to him, his fangs broke through.

"What are you doing?" He growled at Benji.

"Sarah's gone!" Benji screamed at the top of his lungs in a panic. Tiny blood drops began to roll down his face. He was crying for her, the revelation that a vampire harbors true love for his mate. Cam has only cried once for me as far as I know.

"What are we going to do?" Benji yelled out.

Cam grabbed a hold of Benji's shoulders and calmly turned him around to face the entryway.

"I'm not missing, Benji. My dad showed up here this morning. I let you sleep in so I could go visit with him for a while." Sarah stood with her heels together, a long pink dress flowed down to her ankles. She was flawless as expected when she's in Wesley's presence.

The two embraced. I broke out into a fit of tears.

I looked over at Cam, still in his boxers and groggy having been suddenly awakened. I could see the gears in his mind winding, trying to figure out exactly what happened. I began to laugh as I continued to cry.

"See what you've done." Cam wrapped his arms around me and patted my back. "There, there, now my sweetheart."

"Where is your father?" Cam asked Sarah while holding me.

"In Rayan's study." Sarah replied, raising her head up from Benji's shoulder long enough to get her words out. "Cam, he's very upset with me. Could you please talk to him?" She said. "He knows everything about the Sharon situation and to top that off, he knows Benji, and I now share a room." She tried to speak as properly and grownup as possible.

"Oh." Cam chuckled. "The two of you need to occupy yourselves with something productive, out of sight, out of mind is best right now." Cam said.

Sarah curtsied and smiled before leaving the room with her love.

Cam kissed me on the forehead. "I'm going to go talk to Wesley." He stood up, buttoned his slacks, and grabbed his white collared shirt from the chair.

"I'm going with you." I said. He didn't disagree.

I could see that Wesley was in vampire form before we entered the Study.

"Do you still want to go in?" Cam raised his eyebrows and gave me a sideways look.

"Yeah." I wasn't scared of Wesley.

"I knew I should have made Sharon and Ken leave as soon as I brought Sarah home. Sharon is no part of me. She is a liability to this group." He spoke towards Cam. "Oh, excuse me, Marry." He finally realized I was in the room. He quickly retracted his fangs. "Normally I would have caught myself and corrected my rudeness but right now I am beyond angry."

"I understand, Wesley." I smiled.

"How do you want me to handle this, Wesley?" Cam asked. He was ready to go and do whatever he needed to do to defend Sarah and Wesley.

"I thought about sending you, son but I am going to take care of this, myself." Wesley said.

I silently wished I could be there to watch this unfold.

"Shouldn't I come with you?" Cam said.

"No, you stay here with Marry. I'm aware she's with child. That became obvious when you left Marry's prescription for prenatal vitamins in my room back at the hospital. I told Dr. Patak to tell me once the results were back in, and we knew for a fact that she was pregnant. Don't get upset with him. He reports to me first, always." Wesley smiled.

"Rayan is headed to Colorado now. He and I will discuss and handle this whole thing to where it shall never be a problem again." Wesley's face straightened as a look of disappointment covered Cam's. "You're Marry's husband, first. What the two of you are about to bring into this world will forever secure the EVG's position as it is ranked. Your job here is much more important." Wesley said.

I felt a heat come over me. He referred to our child as a what. I wasn't sure how to feel about that.

"I would, however, like for the two of you to take Benji and Sarah back to Charlotte with you today and leave as soon as possible - Travel by car. I know the trip will be long but more secure. I have arranged a special driver for the four of you. If you agree." Wesley said.

"Yes!" We both said in sync. We would do anything to keep Sarah and Benji safe.

"I hope I don't fail to show my gratitude for the way you are looking after Skylar and have always kept my family as a priority in your own lives. This hasn't gone unnoticed." Wesley was a good man to say the least – I'd never been given a reason to believe otherwise.

"Jerome is here now to chauffer you." Wesley reached his hand out to shake Cam's. "I have decided to bless the two of you and with what will remain unknown until the appropriate time and place. It will be a joyous reward." He then took my hand and kissed it.

Neither Cam nor I questioned the gift.

"Take care of my family, son." Wesley said to Cam on

our way out the door.

"Take care of yourself, old man." Cam replied, laughing.

The four of us loaded into a Cadillac Escalade, the third-row seating was necessary. I was glad that Jerome agreed to be our driver for this trip. He was the best vampire for the job. I hated our romantic getaway was cancelled but now knowing grandmother was in Charlotte, alone, with Skylar, I was anxious to get back there.

When we finally stopped, we realized how quiet the back seat had become. Sarah and Benji were sharing a very intimate kiss. All Cam could do to get them to stop was cough loudly. "Save that stuff for another time." He told them.

They were young at heart. The vivid memories of how my love for Cam began swept over me. I took a deep breath.

CHAPTER 19

I stared up at the Maple and Poplar trees that scattered our property. My feet crunched across the fallen leaves. The ones left hanging on the branches were of the most beautiful colors, yellows, and reds. I loved this time of year. I began to think about the holidays and how whenever I felt sad, scared, or anxious, my mother would tell me to dream about Christmas. There was never a time that didn't bring me joy. I now had pleasant visions of our baby, Cam, and I sitting around the Christmas tree, the bright multicolored lights sparkling throughout the room.

"Elizabeth's in trouble!" Benji yelled from right inside the door. It was the first time I witnessed his vampire senses in action. I wasn't sure if he had any before this.

Cam, Sarah and Benji, fangs out, ran down the hall towards Skylar's room. I followed as quickly as I could. The closer I got, the more pronounced a struggle became, a loud thud against the wall proved the commotion was indeed coming from Skylar's room. When I made it inside, Cam had grandmother in his arms. Blood gushing from her neck. I dropped to my knees.

"Grandmother, please Lord - No!" I cried out.

She slowly reached her hand up, it was then I knew she was still alive.

"Did you change her?" I screamed towards Cam.

"No, this is not a bite! Her neck has been sliced." He hissed back.

Screeching noises came from inside the living room followed by glass shattering. Rayan flew through Skylar's door having felt my grandmother injured. He immediately took her from Cam's arms. Cam disappeared. Blood puddled underneath Rayan's feet as grandmother's skin became a gruesome pale. Rayan tightened his grip on her. I knew she was dying.

"Elizabeth, I love you!" Rayan struggled to get his

words out. "I can save you if you allow me." He cried. "Blink once if you will submit to a forever and always life with me." He begged her as blood drops rolled down his face.

She closed her eyes and held them shut for what seemed like an eternity. When she finally did open them, she stared at him, refusing to blink any further. He gave her the gift of immortality right there in front of me. Rayan hurried past me, carrying grandmother.

"What about Cam?" I whispered to him.

"What about Cam? He's doing exactly what should have been done, what he's been waiting to do. Check the back porch whenever you are ready to see him." Rayan said.

I had become so concerned with grandmother, I didn't look for Skylar, none of us had. I heard a small voice.

"Marry, I'm okay." The closet door slowly opened and wrapped in numerous blankets; Skylar appeared without a scratch on him. "Uncle Cam and Uncle Rayan knew I was safe, that's why they didn't look for me." Skylar said. It was then I knew he could read minds. I hugged him tightly until Nurse Randy nudged me out of the way.

"Move miss, we must evaluate the boy." Nurse Randy said.

I stood dumbfounded for a moment, wondering how the nurse could use such a tone with me. I left the room and went to find Cam. The hallway felt longer than usual and abnormally dark. I rounded the corner searching for my husband. I quickly took a step back when I heard the crunch of broken glass underneath my feet, the patio windows had been shattered and the doors stood wide open.

A repeated thud from the outside caught my attention. I looked to find Cam in full vampire suit. He had Sharon in his grip forcing her body over the wood railing, punching her repeatedly in the throat. She let out the most horrifying, pitchy squawk I had ever heard. The old me would have felt sorry for her but I now held zero tolerance for one such as her. Feeling my presence, Cam turned to look at me. His face, covered in blood and his eyes full of detestation. He spoke to me as he continued to strike her. "All this broad had going for her was her speed. She was a fast-little tramp." He growled.

He leaned down and began to gnaw on her neck until her head detached from her body introducing her to true death. Her body decomposed right there in a matter of seconds. The wind swooshed around, the clouds swirled, and lightning began to strike. The pink dress Sharon once wore was now blowing uncontrollably in the wind. Cam screamed out in agony, but it wasn't a pain at all. The screech was so piercing, I dropped to my knees and covered my face, the strength of the wind accelerated, I became immobile.

Sharon's body disproportionately gathered itself back together.

Cam stared into the storm as if it were a pair of discerning eyes.

A howling force spun violently down, lifting Sharon, and removing her corpse, carrying her off into the upper parts of the unknown. Sharon was no more. Immediately the harsh elements ceased.

I could feel his presence and hear his voice "I don't want you to see me like this, Marry." He said. All I could see of him were his black leather boots crunching over the broken glass. I had no choice but to wait for his return.

I sat down on the sofa, pulling my legs underneath me.

Nurse Randy walked by, stopping to speak. "Marry, the wind from that pop-up storm has left the air a little cool. Maybe you should move away from the open area." Referring to the empty space that windows once occupied.

"Cover up with this blanket if you must continue to sit there." She gently laid the covers across my lap. She began to walk off just as a thought crossed my mind.

"Randy, where were you when this whole thing started?

Where was Skylar's medical team when Sharon entered the house?" I asked.

"Me, Grace and Dr. Patak plus your grandmother were all here. We're not sure how she got in without tripping any alarms, but she did. His medical team, including myself were meeting to discuss further treatment options for Skylar." She hung her head in shame. "We've all been trained to recognize Sharon and what to do if she were to appear. But I promise you, Mrs. Marry, none of us knew and we can't understand it. It was your grandmother that realized something was off. She went to Skylar, saving him by helping him into the closet. It was by the grace of God that you all showed up when you did, or your grandmother would have surely perished and quite likely Skylar and the rest of us would have too. If anything good came from this, it was realizing just how strong your grandmother is! I only wish to be so brave! I'm sorry this happened." Randy shook her head.

It was a compliment for a vampire to admire my grandmother's will while she was still human.

Now seemed as perfect a time as any for me to address her subtle roughness with me when she finally did enter the room to check on Sklyar. Randy's display of niceness allowed me to cease my thoughts of telling Cam. She deserved to live, now.

I stood up from where I was sitting so I could look her directly in the eyes. "Randy." I said.

"Ma'am?" She replied.

"I feel that I cannot go without bringing this to your attention, for the sake of..." I paused. "...Our friendship, I suppose." I continued.

Her eyes squinted slightly as she looked in my direction. Her neck began to pulsate rapidly.

"Oh, you poor thing. You're nervous." I reached up and placed my fingertips over the throb. "You were a little rough with me when you finally entered the room to assist

Skylar." My words were drawn out, I could feel the anger boiling within me, something I would normally choose to ignore.

The whites of her eyes started bubbling with red, her veins forming paths of blood.

"You're angry?" I calmly asked.

Her pointed fangs meant to scare me only intensified my new feeling. "Cam!" I let out an earth-shattering scream summoning my husband. "As the woman of this house, I will not be made to feel any other way than queen. Capiche?" I said.

Cam whisked by me and carried Randy to her demise.

He tiredly dragged his feet as he made his way back in the house. "For the love of everything vampire, can you please go take a nap or something?" He scolded me as he headed back up the stairs to our quarters. I thumbed through a magazine, smiling. Our bond would never be broken, especially now with his baby growing inside of me.

CHAPTER 20

I peeked in on Skylar who was napping. Cam startled me when he grabbed me from behind, spinning me around to face him. He began to kiss each bare section of my body, forehead, cheeks, neck, hands, wrists. "I apologize for everything you observed yesterday, my love. I hate that you had to witness me in the most horrifying of states."

"What will happen to you for killing one of your own? I'm aware of what and who you are, clearly, but I have found myself worried about what was done to Sharon and if you could possibly face repercussions. Oh yeah, and Randy too." I sighed then leaned into him.

He wrapped his arms tightly around me, lifting me gently from the floor. He carried me further down the hall. "I will not have to answer for my actions, love." He lovingly looked into my eyes.

"I can tell you this, Sharon was a very fast-moving vampire, that was her strength and now that I have fed on her to the point of no return, by her being EVG, her blood mixed with mine will only give me an increased speed. I'm not exactly sure how fast as of now but I'm sure to find out soon. And regarding Randy, probably not much there for me but who knows, maybe I'll be a nurse." He laughed loudly, tickling my funny bone. We both stood there laughing uncontrollably. I held my stomach to try and stop it from shaking like a bowl full of jelly.

We both took a few deep breaths.

"But because Sharon was Skylar's mother, I believe he and I will be more closely connected. That couldn't hurt." He said.

I looked around the house, it was destroyed, in a desperate state of disarray. I wanted to move past all this, but I couldn't with my home in shambles. "Who's going to clean up all this mess and fix the broken glass?" No quicker than the words exited my mouth, there was a knock at the door.

"Clean-up crew." Cam looked at me and smiled.

"They fix windows and clean, too?" I asked.

"Yes! Let's go play video games with Skylar. They're going to fix his window first and I want to be in there while they do." Cam said.

Skylar grinned massively when we walked through the door. Cam excused Cherry from her nurse duties and picked up a controller from Skylar's nightstand. He taunted Skylar with it. "You want to test your skills, little boy?" Cam laughed.

"You don't have anything on me, Uncle Cam." Skylar's tone was a bit more serious.

"Alright, okay." Cam sat down in the giant hand chair before quickly jumping back up.

"Marry, take a hand." He laughed. "Okay, you take the seat." He laughed again.

I shook my head no and crawled up in the bed next to Skylar. "You're the one that's going to need a hand." I laughed and watched as both of their teams entered onto the field, football was the choice, not really my forte.

Skylar was as comfortable as I had ever seen him. He began to open up about his mother. He still had no idea that she was the one that had been trying to hurt him this whole time. He knew someone was trying to hurt him, but he couldn't understand why, none of us could fully understand.

He told us how his mother had once brought his Uncle Stevie to see him in the hospital. That touched a nerve with Cam. His ears pointed immediately upward as they sometimes did in deep conversations.

Skylar said he liked his Uncle Stevie, he was funny, kind, and talked weird, referring to his country accent.

"Another man came with her once, and it wasn't Ken." Skylar said. "He was a tall, skinny man and he looked old. Mom said they were friends but the way he cried when he looked at me gave me the creeps. He hugged me tight and then tried to kiss me on the cheek, I pulled away. I didn't want a stranger putting his lips on me." Skylar stuck his tongue out and made an icky noise.

"Momma liked the man a lot. I could tell by the way she kept smiling at him and rubbing up his arm trying to make him feel better when really, I was the one upset."

"Are you hearing this?" I whispered to Cam.

"I am." Cam said.

Cam took the video game controller from Skylar's hands and placed it down on the table next to him. "Did your mom ever tell you his name, buddy?" Skylar was so trusting and that wasn't always a good thing.

"She said his name was Shelly, Shelby, Shelbon, I can't remember. I'm sorry, Uncle Cam." He said.

"No need to be sorry, buddy. I was just wondering if I knew him." Cam said. He picked the controller back up and continued with the game. His eyes focused blankly on the screen, but I knew he was thinking the same thing I was. Shelton was Skylar's father. Shelton tried to play Cam the night he and Sharon were at the restaurant in Memphis. Shelton told the truth about what she wanted from him but what he didn't mention is her request of him was not that far-fetched and at the end of the day all this does is prove Shelton too did not care if his own son, Skylar was going to be murdered or not.

I couldn't hold it in any longer. "Cam, can I see you in the hall?" I said.

He kicked his feet like a kid, pretending to be upset about my request that would pull him from his game. "Be right back, Sky." Cam said.

Once out of the room, he pulled me close to him. He looked down at me, staring directly into my eyes. "I know your mind is running a million miles a minute. But it's all cut and dry. It is what is." He said.

"So, Shelton is Skylar's father and when he and Sharon

found out that Wesley knew - they came up with a plan to kill Skylar and rid themselves of their dirty little secret." I calmly spoke in an attempt to keep from screaming. "All that talk he did about never cheating on his sweet Betsy! Lies!" I formed a fist.

"Yep, he's a real piece of work." Cam said. "He'll be done away with. I've planned his demise ever since our first meeting." He smirked.

"What are you talking about, Cam?" I asked.

"I wanted to take him out that night he was in the car with us, but I didn't, because during our time in Memphis working with Dr. Patak on breeding issues, I met Shelton's second in command. He is not much older than me and has a human wife nearly as young as you. The two of them are also trying to conceive. He and his wife have just moved to the United States from British Columbia. He told me a lot more than I would have expected but I guess that's what men do when they are waiting to see a doctor to extract seed from them." He laughed but was obviously serious.

"He and his wife had to come here at the direction of VAM's council. Shelton is under investigation for treason. I believe VAM knows about Skylar, too. I'm curious to see how this is going to unfold." Cam smirked.

I gasped at the news. "Who is this guy and why would he volunteer that information?" I asked.

"His name is Loren, from what I can tell, he seems like a pretty decent guy. I don't understand his trustworthiness. That's why I treat every situation as some sort of setup. I can't be outsmarted." He hissed in my direction, picked me up and took me away.

"Feed me." He didn't laugh or give me any reason to think he was joking. I knew he wouldn't overindulge because whatever he took from me, he also took from our baby.

CHAPTER 21

The winter months came and went. My stomach was so large now that Cam took me shopping nearly weekly.

"You're kind of large for five months." Dr. Patak sulked at my weight gain but never offered any advice on how to slow it. Cam liked the extra pounds on me and as long as he was happy, I was happy.

Cam and I ended up making friends with Loren and his human wife, Avery, who was now two months pregnant. She and I were making vampire history. We were both excited but scared, unsure of the future. I had a due date of late July, early August and hers was somewhere around the end of October.

Cam was spending a lot of his time at home with me, and I was thankful for that. We had lived pretty drama free for the past couple of months but there was still nothing boring about our lives.

My grandmother was adapting to her new role as vampire. It was becoming of her. She looked like she had gone back in time by at least ten years. She had always been a beautiful creature but to see her now was amazing! Her looks almost made me want to make the change myself.

Skylar was making progress but still needed an extra amount of VAM DNA to get where he needed to be health wise.

The whole Shelton situation and the fact that we now knew he was Skylar's dad hadn't been addressed. Loren went to Wesley and asked that we keep that under wraps for the sake of the inquiry that was being made into Shelton by his own group.

Since Cam had become rather well acquainted with Loren, Wesley called a meeting with him and Rayan and let them have the final say so. They both agreed the secret would be kept until further notice. After all, the best way to handle Shelton would be his own people killing him verses any of EVG doing it even though Cam would've found great joy in introducing Shelton to his final death.

Ken didn't stir up any mess when he found out Sharon was dead. He barely asked any questions. I think a burden had been lifted off him. He didn't get angry when they told him Skylar was not his son. No one ever disclosed that bit of heartbreaking information to Skylar because he had already suffered so many great losses in his life. He was told that Ken was going away on business and his visits would be few and far between. Cam offered to pay Ken for his return annually to see Skylar and show him some fatherly love - Ken wouldn't accept his money but agreed that he would make the trip out of love for Skylar.

"Boo!" Cam startled me out of my deep thoughts.

"Do not scare a pregnant woman, Cam!" I turned and fussed at him.

He kissed me softly on the jaw and handed me my jacket. "Let's go check on Stevie. The ride will do us both some good." He said.

"It's beautiful!" From the road, I could see that the old raggedy home had been painted yellow, the shutters were now a bright, clean white. Its magnificence glowed throughout the land.

"That boy's something else. isn't he?" Cam chuckled at the brilliant new look.

Stevie was standing out by the shed when he realized we were headed his way. He raised his hand to wave.

"Cam, Mrs. Marry" Stevie tilted his hat towards us.

"Dear Lord, Stevie. What did you do to the house?" I asked.

Cam kicked a little dirt with his shoe, staring at the ground, all the while smiling.

"I hope it's okay with y'all." He said. A look of concern formed on his face.

"Boy, you know I told you to do whatever you wanted

with this old place as long as you kept your mind free and clear from all those substances." Cam said.

Stevie's smile spread from one side of his face to the other.

"I'm glad you two are here." Stevie took off towards the house. "I have something for y'all and It's probably going to blow your mind but when I tell ya' that something told me to do this, something told me to do this! I had another one of them dreams. They used to scare me but now I realize they're just speaking to me. It's a form of communication - from who or what, I don't know though." Stevie motioned for us to follow him.

"Ladies first." He waved his hand in front of me and then pretended to punch Cam in the arm. "You just don't know what y'all done for me, Cam. You saved my life. I owe you everything, man. Like I told you last time you were here - I ain't never going back to my old ways. I know it in my heart, and I have seen myself doing even better than this, Cam - In those dreams I have." Stevie sighed in relief as we walked through the back door.

There in the corner sat another cradle just like the first one Stevie made for us. "Stevie, you already gave us one of these, no need for another one." I spoke quickly, afraid of what he might be insinuating.

Cam brought his hand up to his forehead and wiped the sweat from his brow.

"Oh, but Mrs. Marry, I do believe there is a reason for this second baby bed." Stevie said.

"Why on earth would you say that?" I yelled. Then all the signs began to play though my head, extreme weight gain, extraordinary moodiness, the list went on and on. Panic set in when I heard Wesley's voice. "I'm going to bless you both with a precious gift. Two is better than one." That's exactly what he said!

Cam called my name over and over again. I didn't hear anything until finally I did.

"What?" I screamed.

"What is wrong with you?" He asked.

"I know what's wrong with her." Stevie said.

"Shut up, Stevie!" Cam and I said simultaneously.

I immediately apologized to Stevie, not wanting to do anything to crush his spirits. "Stevie, did you dream I was having twins? Did you?" I asked him.

"Yes ma'am, I did. I'm sorry." Stevie picked at his fingernails.

I stormed out of the house, both Cam and Stevie followed me.

"Cam, did you know this? Did Wesley tell you he was going to do this? That's something you just don't go around doing, you know? Messing with a woman's body and all. Nobody had the right! Nobody!" I screamed, waving a fist at him.

"First of all, I don't know what Wesley would have to do with any of this, Marry! Second of all, if we are having twins then we're having twins and there's nothing you or anyone else can do about it. That's just a double blessing. I understand you being in shock. Truthfully, I hope it is twins but Dr. Patak showed us the sonogram. There's only one baby. So, calm down. Take a few deep breaths." Cam encouraged me, stress wasn't good for me or the baby.

Cam was right, the sonogram showed only one and a dream is just a dream. There were no facts to support twins. I began to laugh hysterically at the thought. Once I laughed, Stevie and Cam began to laugh. Yeah, everything was fine. I was sure of it.

"Thank you very much, Stevie! Your woodwork is beyond gorgeous! You should really think about selling some of your creations." I walked to the car, slamming the door shut once I was in.

"Her hormones are out of control. It's all good, my man. We can always use it in another room. Appreciate you, brother." Cam said as quickly got behind the wheel of the car.

"Look, I don't know anything about you having twins. We can have Dr. Patak do another ultrasound, okay? Confirm that you are just carrying one baby." He said.

"No need. I know I'm carrying two babies. I feel it in my heart. Let me think what I want to think. I'm just trying to make it through this pregnancy. I want to go home and go to sleep. I'm tired. But somebody needs to take the truck back down there because we are going to need that second bed." I said.

I stared quietly out the window the entire trip back.

"Carry me to my bed, Cam." I insisted once we arrived home. I figured he needed to do some of the work where these babies were concerned. And, he's going to be the one getting up in the middle of the night with them. I sighed, realizing that wouldn't be an issue for him.

This is so unfair.

I wanted Cam to ask Wesley about the second baby - to see if maybe he had paid for Dr. Patak to gift us a second child but then if he hadn't that would make things a little awkward for all of us.

Cam carried me up to bed and laid me down gently. He took off my shoes and socks and began to rub my feet. I'm surprised he didn't know by now; this was not something I found enjoyable. I was extremely ticklish, the more he rubbed the more I kicked and laughed!

"Stop Cam! I can't take it!" I tried to tell him, but my words were muzzled by laughter and when I kicked at him, the baby kicked too. I raised my shirt, showing off my belly. "Look, Cam!" I said.

He reached over to rub my stomach and that's when all became known. Both babies kicked and with both legs, causing four little indentions to poke through my tummy. They kicked over and over again, my stomach raising with their every move. I rubbed my hand over them, they were powerful little somethings. Cam placed his hand over mine and began to speak to his offsprings.

"Daddy loves you, babies. You will never want for anything." Two single tear drops of blood fell upon my stomach, stains that I would never be able to remove. This type of love was unimaginable to me and now that I knew for sure there were twins, I was no longer upset.

"Mommy loves you more." I spoke to them hoping to make Cam jealous.

He smiled, cut his eyes towards me, and pulled me in closer to him. "All three of daddy's babies." He spoke softly.

I laid my head on his chest. It was true, I was daddy's baby, too.

CHAPTER 22

Dr. Patak finally had a sonogram machine delivered to Charlotte and today we would find out the sex of the babies. I could hardly contain my excitement.

My grandmother decided to sit in on this visit. "I don't know how he doesn't see that second baby." She exclaimed.

Ever since her transition from human to vampire she was much more boisterous and bossier, just how Rayan liked her. They were more in love than ever, now. Something I didn't think was possible for the two.

"I'm sure he will see two, today." I told her.

She shook her head and smirked.

Cam sat still and quiet in anticipation.

Dr. Patak entered the room and greeted us all. "What is this I hear about a second baby?" Dr. Patak asked.

"A second baby that my wife and mother-in-law feel you should have seen a long time before now, doc" Cam said. "I mimic their feelings." Cam raised his brows.

"Marry, undress and put on this gown. I will be back in in just a moment to see what we have going on in there." He gave us a nod as he left the room.

Cam assisted me with the gown and then lifted me atop the table. I had gained so much weight that I probably wouldn't have made it up there otherwise.

He looked at me with adoring eyes and all I could think about was a cheeseburger dressed with lettuce, tomato, and mayonnaise and how maybe I could get Cherry to make me some homemade French fries to go with it. I wiped my mouth when I realized I had begun to drool.

This was my story as a pregnant woman.

Dr. Patak came back into the room and introduced me to his new nurse. She was an older lady, probably in her late sixties. She wore her hair in a bun, no makeup and her skirt hung way past her knees. I liked her already.

"This is Nurse Bertha. She is my new assistant." He

said, right before he turned off the lights. Bertha stood next to me like a guard as Dr. Patak squirted the cold blue gel on my belly. I cringed at the chill. He began to move what I call the magic wand all around my stomach until he came up with baby number one. "Do you see that?" He circled an area on the screen. "Your baby is a boy!" Dr. Patak said.

"Yes, I knew it." I was overjoyed. "Now find the other one, doctor." I told him.

He continued the search for baby number two, but he still didn't find anything.

"How is that possible?" I screamed at the man.

"This doctor has no clue what he's doing! Cam, you need to obtain the equivalent of Dr. Spock to care for my granddaughter. This guy is beginning to work my nerves." My grandmother said angrily as she got up and exited the room.

Dr. Patak searched and searched with his magic wand but never located a second baby. We left the appointment with medical facts of a single child, but I wasn't convinced, and neither was Cam. We were quite aware that we were expecting two babies.

I did a lot of baby shopping with Avery. Cam and Loren followed us around the stores like bodyguards and rightfully so. It was truly like something from the movies. People smiled and stared as we waddled along with our big tummies, picking whatever we liked for our babies, no limits on anything.

As time went on, I became more fatigued and less likely to participate in any activities outside of the home. I helped Cam set up the nursery for our baby boy whom we decided to call Cameron Marcel Rosenthal.

Not long after that, Loren was sent on a mission to stop Shelton from breaking into a safe VAM had secured in Maine. Shelton intended on taking all the cash and somehow blaming the EVG's for the heist. Wesley and Rayan allowed Cam to accompany Loren since EVG would be named as the culprits. Loren leaked that bit of information to Cam, also.

Cam had built a seemingly tight relationship with Loren. Everyone seemed to like the guy but as Cam always said - trust no one. He was also a firm believer in keeping your friends close and your enemies closer. He claimed to have no friends, only family. That was true for all of us, I suppose. If we had friends at all, I guess Loren and Avery would hold that title.

Avery and I stayed at home, eating snacks, and thumbing through baby magazines. We spoke about all the dreams we had for the little ones that would soon join our families. I couldn't have imagined anything going wrong that night. But now that I think back, we were all a little foolish in thinking that Shelton was blind to what was going on around him. He knew he was being followed but he chose to go on with his plans to take the money. He wasn't the only crook in his group. It was known he had a team but still, sometimes we let our pride and status get in the way of reality.

Shelton was a self-destructive vampire to say the least and after the true death of Sharon - his suicide mission had become more evident to the ones around him. He was willing to take himself out and anyone else in his way.

Both groups became aware that Sharon was and had been Shelton's only true love.

The mistake that set all these events into motion occurred the night that Sharon and Stevie were changed. Shelton's intention had always been to have Sharon as VAM but Read got to her first.

Loren and Cam formed a crew to go in and stop Shelton's plan, to fully expose him and his schemes and of course to keep EVG's name faultless.

Things didn't go as planned. Shelton walked into his headquarters as he normally would and went directly to the vault but what happened next is what sent everyone scrambling. Shelton had one of his drivers back a Semi truck directly through the building - it ran over many of his employees, some which we know to have been human.

Cam and Loren ran in to try and stop the bloody massacre, but it was too late. The unexpected won. The impact wasn't strong enough to kill the vampires inside, but it took the lives of many mortal beings and just as Shelton planned all along, his ploy got the reaction out of Loren that he had hoped for. Shelton desired the chase. He wanted the confrontation with Loren, an opportunity to battle his second in command, one on one, hoping to destroy Loren.

Rayan took the call the night that Cam ended up in a VAM jail but worse than that Loren had been killed during the vampire raid Shelton conducted on his own people.

Shelton grabbed a sword from behind his leather cloak and beheaded anyone in his reach. Loren succumbed to the laceration of such a powerful object - The knife and Shelton - One no greater than the other but both required to succeed at such a catastrophic deed.

What Shelton didn't know and never would have expected is that Cam was with Loren.

Cam's black leather boots contained a sharp metal plate that ejected when prompted. With the speed Cam gained from Sharon, he swiftly approached Shelton and with a roll kick, sliced his immortal throat but only enough to cause physical harm not death. Cam moved in so quickly, Shelton couldn't comprehend what had transpired.

In Shelton's attempt to regain his composure, Cam snagged Shelton's own sword from him and beheaded the selfish VAM leader with one mighty blow. Cam could only describe the devastation as great.

Cam told how he couldn't walk away, that he had no choice but to burn the place down, making sure Shelton met his final death.

The VAM vampires left living became disorientated and flew frantically over the building avoiding the flames, some hovered and screamed in agony as they watched their leader burn to death – Members of VAM didn't freeze at the sight of fire like an EVG would have. Their torment merely came from the pain and suffering they could feel Shelton experiencing. Most of them were unaware of the pending charges against Shelton.

Cam burned it all, the corpses, the money Shelton was willing to give his life for, the entire building went up in flames.

I was angry that Cam risked his own life to bring final death upon Shelton.

My heart hurt so badly for Avery and for Shelton's own wife, Betsy, all the things she learned that day must've devastated her.

Evil always begets evil.

When members of VAM's council arrived, they had instructions to take Cam into custody. It was protocol and Wesley gave his permission for them to do so.

Wesley and Rayan were already on their way to me when I got the news. I knew then that we would go get him as soon as they arrived. He was being held in a cell and under no distress. They assured me of this and I knew that if anything had gone wrong, Wesley and Rayan would have already torn that place down.

We all agreed that we wouldn't tell Avery about Loren until we had Cam back at home with us. All she knew was the two of them had gotten into an altercation of some sort and that Wesley, Rayan and I were going to Maine to see what exactly was going on. They took me with them because leaving me at home was never going to be an option I would agree to.

I wasn't afraid when we arrived. Wesley spoke to the person in charge, handed over a wad of money and then Cam was released to us.

Cam pulled his pants up from the waist, kicked his boots

out to the side and hissed at everyone in his path. I felt like his mouth would swallow me whole the way he kissed me.

I could finally breathe again having him back by my side.

"I need to get to a shower, as soon as possible. I'm covered in VAM juice." Cam said.

Wesley turned and gave him a quick grin.

We traveled back just the way we came. Rayan lifted me in his arms and off we flew. Cam didn't feel comfortable carrying me such a distance after the strenuous events of the night.

CHAPTER 23

Steam from the shower spiraled out from underneath the bathroom door and into the bedroom.

The room was filled with silence as the minutes went by, my heart sank. I forced my big self up from the bed and made my way to the door. I grasped the knob thinking twice before entering.

I quietly opened the door to see him with his head leaned against the tile, the hot water pouring down the back of his neck and further.

Feeling my presence, he leaned up and looked at me. His face red from tears.

"Cam." With all my clothes on, I got in behind him and wrapped my arms tightly around his wet body.

"I don't ever want to lose you." He said. He then began to remove my drenched clothing. He rubbed his hand gently over my stomach, moving down to repeat his words to our offspring.

"How did you keep from being frozen by the fire?" I asked, rubbing his hair away from his face.

He looked at me with understanding and tired eyes. "I was in no danger, with the extra speed I now possess, I was able to flee harm's way before I even felt the heat." He guided me from the shower, took a towel from the rack and dried me off.

"I'm glad it's over but I'm so sorry about the heartache that Avery will have to endure. None of us expected Shelton to go as far as he did." He hung his head in what appeared to be shame.

I understood how he felt, and how devastating this would be for Avery and her unborn baby.

"Avery can stay here until she is ready to go." Cam said.

I agreed to a month at the most, not because I lacked empathy for Avery and the baby but because my grandmother had taught me many things over the years, including always keep other women away from your man. I trusted Cam but I know how the world turns, and I know who stirs it up enough to make it go in a circular motion – Women, nothing more, nothing less.

We still hadn't delivered the news to Avery about Loren. Wesley calmed her with a spell so that she would rest until the time was right if there was ever such a time.

Cam needed rest. He held me tightly as he dozed off. Once I knew he was sleeping, I got up and watched him. His chest moved up and down as if his lungs filled with air. I wasn't sure that was the case though. What I did know was he was the most handsome creature in existence.

"Woah." I whispered hoping not to wake Cam. The baby had given me a harsh kick. I rubbed my stomach to try and sooth him, but he wouldn't stop. I leaned over towards him as far as I could and again, softly spoke. "Son, you will one day be a great leader, there will be no other before you." I wasn't sure what made me speak those words.

Cam abruptly jumped up from his sleep, wide eyed he gasped for breath. "He told her."

"What?" I said.

"He told her about Loren. Wesley told her about Loren." He said.

It became so quiet that even I could now hear her wails of sorrow.

"Go to her, Marry." Cam said as he chose to stay still in the moment.

I went down the steps and looked in on her, Wesley sat next to her, allowing her to grieve. He stood up and moved to the chair in the corner. I took his previous seat.

"Avery." I said.

Her pregnant body didn't budge from its curled up fetal position on the oversized bed. I knew there weren't any words of comfort that I could say. I merely sat there, through the night, Wesley and I sat there.

The sun began to peep through the dark colored blinds. Tears no longer fell from Avery's eyes though her crying had not ceased. Wesley rubbed both of his pointer fingers in a straight line over them, immediately the noise stopped. He had managed to put her in a deep sleep. I was amazed by his actions, having never seen that done before in all the years I had been part of this group.

"Cherry has breakfast ready for you in the dining room. Cam awaits you there." Wesley instructed. "There's nothing you can do for her at this time. I will have Dr. Patak feed her intravenously, so the child gets the nutrients it needs to survive. She too will live through this suffering. Cherry will remain with her while I sleep. Go to your husband, Marry."

I nodded and left the room.

Cam sat at the table reading the daily news. He shook the paper, folded it, and greeted me. "Hello, my lovely wife." He patted the chair next to him. "Sit." He said.

I could barely muster up a smile, but I knew none of this was Cam's fault.

He placed his hand on my stomach, the baby went wild.

"He's been kicking a lot for the past couple of days but nothing like this." I put my hand over Cams.

"He knows his daddy." I said.

Cam glared at me angrily. "Always daddy!"

"What is that about, Cam?" I yelled, causing Wesley to enter the room.

"Cam, is there a problem?" Wesley scoffed.

"None!" Cam's single word caused Wesley to scold him and pull him to the side. I couldn't hear what they were saying, I could only see that Cam's attitude began to lighten as he reapproached me.

"I'm sorry, my love, with everything that has gone on lately, infidelities of both vampire and human, I felt the need to offer you a friendly reminder that I will kill you should you ever make a bad decision of that sort." Cam said.

Wesley's neck snapped in a quick response to Cam's words.

Cam began to laugh as if he were joking but Wesley and I both knew otherwise.

"I'll kill you too should you do anything against me." My statement lacked the scare his came with.

CHAPTER 24

I gently tapped on Avery's slightly open bedroom door. "Knock, knock. Can I come in?" I said.

Cherry welcomed me into the room. "Mrs. Marry."

"Hello, Cherry. I wanted to stop by and check on momma bear." I said.

Cherry's solemn smile gave clue to Avery's condition. Avery was still in bed, her eyes open but she didn't mutter a sound. I took the cold wet rag from the nightstand and rubbed her forehead with it.

"Is she still not eating?" I asked Cherry.

"Not a bite." She replied.

I stayed with her for at least two hours, not being much help to Avery or Cherry, I decided to leave. I placed a loving kiss on Avery's forehead and began to walk out. As soon as I turned towards the door, Avery weakly grabbed my hand. I could feel her lack of strength from the frail touch.

"Avery." I placed my hand on top of hers.

She began to speak but her words were unable to form through the tears. My heart broke for her. I tried to reassure her that everything would be okay. I knew that meant little or nothing to her. Cam blamed himself but there was nothing anyone could have done. We didn't know Avery or Loren before all this happened and I can only imagine that VAM would've lost a lot more had Cam decided not to involve himself in the takedown of Shelton. EVG had reason to want Shelton gone - not only because of Skylar but because of so many more crimes he had committed. His lies couldn't be numbered.

Cam and Rayan took a day trip to Rhode Island to make sure everything in grandmother's house was secure. It had been unoccupied for so long, they wanted to be sure no rodents of mankind or creepy crawly creatures had decided to form nests anywhere on the property.

I worked on Cameron's nursery making sure I had everything I would need for our new arrival. Both bassinets created by Stevie sat mid room against the wall. I figured I would give the second one to Avery closer to her delivery time. Rayan still laughs about the fact that he made us two of them. Rayan too insists we're having twins but still to this day Dr. Patak only sees one baby on the ultrasound.

The Rocking chair Cam got for me from the Peabody Hotel, the one I envisioned my mother sitting in, cradling Cameron now sat over by the window so I could look out across the land while loving on my bundle.

The room was done in neutral colors since at the time Cam had it decorated, we weren't yet sure the sex of the baby. He offered to redo it in blue, but I liked the yellow and green, reminded me of the bright sunshine and the trees I loved so much. Everything was perfect, the only thing missing was my mother and though I would never admit it, I would've loved for my dad to have been a better vampire and able to teach Cameron some of the thing's grandfathers should teach their grandsons, instead he's trapped below in a training camp with the others whose deeds were unjustifiably cruel.

My grandmother startled me when she spoke. "Is everything okay, Marry?"

"How long have you been standing there?" I asked.

She put her arms around my shoulders and squeezed lightly. "Long enough to know your heart is heavy, child." She sighed. I guess she could read minds like the others, now. I sighed, too.

"Marry, I'm excited for the both of you. You and Cam will make great parents and I must say I'm quite a bit thrilled for myself also, knowing I will have a great grandchild and how much joy the little fella is going to bring to us all." She said. She placed her cold hand around mine and led me to the window. "Look out there, the world is huge, and you have absolutely everything at your fingertips, don't let anyone or anything tell you differently."

We both stood in silence, taking in all the emotions around us.

"The doorbell." Grandmother said.

"I didn't hear anything." I said.

"I'm sure you didn't." She laughed, turning her nose up. "It's Stevie. I can smell a VAM a million miles away."

I nearly gagged at the thought, VAM must stink horribly.

The sun was shining bright, grandmother stood slightly behind me as I opened the door so not to burn.

"Stevie!" I was genuinely happy to see him. "What brings you to our neck of the woods?" I asked.

He tilted his hat to greet us. "Mrs. Marry, Mrs. Rosenthal." He said.

My grandmother didn't like being called Mrs. Rosenthal, made her feel old. "Oh Stevie, just call me Elizabeth." She said. "Come on in."

Stevie was a lot like Tuck, having the ability to stay in the sunlight, one of the reasons he was able to paint the farmhouse so perfectly. He kicked the dirt off his boots and removed his hat, holding it down by his side, before entering our home.

"Is Cam around?" He said. "He asked me to stop by and see him this week, said he had a job for me."

"He's out for a while. He should be back tomorrow. You may want to check in then." I told him.

"Yes ma'am." He politely replied and then began to walk away. Abruptly, he stopped and with vampire quickness, he turned around. His attention now focused on the hallway leading to the bedrooms.

I shook with nervousness, feeling as though something sinister was about to transpire. My trust of others varied.

My grandmother remained calm. I changed positions to see what he was looking at. Cherry had Avery by the arm, walking her to the kitchen.

"She's asked for some real food and wanted to sit at the table." Cherry whispered as she made her way past me.

Stevie's eyes followed her all the way into the dining room. Avery sat down and shyly peeped at the three of us staring at her.

"Mrs. Marry, that's Loren's wife." Stevie knew exactly who he was seeing as he was a member of VAM.

"She's having a tough time about it." I told him.

"I know about Loren's death. I'm saddened for her and their child. Do you think I could have a moment with her." Stevie asked.

I didn't think now was an appropriate time. But Avery, having overheard the conversation insisted now was just as good a time as any.

Stevie still waited for me to give him the okay. "Well, go ahead." I said. "Maybe speaking to you will do her some good."

Stevie was a handsome young man especially now that he had been clean off drugs for so long. Maybe there was a bigger plan in their meeting.

My Grandmother stood nearby, watching, her arms crossed as if Stevie were violating some sort of code by speaking with Avery.

"Stop, grandmother. You look like you're ready to attack someone." I said.

"I just don't care too much for that boy. He isn't anything but a backwoods junkie with a craft." She snipped.

"That was very rude!" I spoke through clenched teeth.

After a few minutes of chatting, Stevie got up and headed towards the door, stopping again to look back at Avery. "Ms. Avery, I imagine we all have to deal with hardships in life and I will be the first to say that the one you are experiencing is far from fair, but I can just image what a wonderful mother you are going to be to that little one. That's a lucky baby you have on the way. If it's alright with you, I would like to bring you something for the baby tomorrow when I come back to see Cam." Stevie's voice was soft, caring but still manly.

Avery looked up from her plate, dabbed her mouth with a napkin, I believe she may have even possessed half a smile. "That would be nice." She said.

He bid us all goodbye and nervously stumbled out the door. "Bye, Ms. Avery." He mumbled once more.

Cameron kicked away at my stomach. Grandmother laughed as she watched his tiny foot make an imprint. "That must be the Cam in him." Grandmother said.

She reached over and gently touched my stomach. He stopped kicking. "He must like you already." I placed my hand on top of hers.

CHAPTER 25

Cam came busting through the door. He flew straight to the downstairs bathroom. I jumped up and followed him. He slammed the door shut before I made it there. I knocked, concerned for his wellbeing.

"What's wrong, Cam?" I spoke through the door.

"I brought you back that Calamari you wanted. That stuff smells horrible! Rayan has it if you're still interested in partaking." He could hardly speak.

"Yum, yes babe. Thank you!" I have been craving Rhode Island fried squid ever since I became pregnant.

Rayan came in carrying the bag and laughing. "Here you go, sweet Marry. We flew back just so your meal wouldn't get old. Your precious husband wanted to make sure you got exactly what you wanted. He tries." Rayan said with a shrug.

I offered some to Avery who was oddly, already up and dressed for the first time since Loren's death. Her face turned an almost grayish color when I asked her if she would like a bite. "Oh, never mind. Y'all don't know what's good! I don't mind eating all of this myself." I dug in.

"Marry, why on earth would you eat that?" My grandmother was also disgusted.

"Come here to me, darling." Rayan said to grandmother, sweeping her up and then carrying her down the hall.

"Okay, bye y'all." Cam said to them, finally making his way back out of the restroom.

It wasn't too long after Rayan and Grandmother vanished from sight into their love nest that we heard a knock at the door. I already knew who it had to be and seeing Avery over there almost back to normal - confirmed it.

"Who is it?" Cam said.

"Cam, It's Stevie. Can you come out here and help me?" He asked.

"Oh Lord, what is this boy up to now?" Cam said.

I shook my head though I knew exactly what he was up to.

Cam opened the door and in the back of Stevie's truck was not a bassinet, but a beautiful crib made of cedar.

"I brought this for Ms. Avery, Cam. I was up the entire night making it. I think it's my masterpiece. What do you think?" I heard him ask Cam.

"Man, that is beautiful. you got skill, you definitely got skill." Cam repeated himself.

I was nearly jealous when they came through the door with it.

Stevie took his hat off as usual when he entered. He spoke to me and then went directly over to Avery. "Good afternoon Ms. Avery." He said.

"Good afternoon, Stevie." She replied with a small grin on her face.

"I made this baby bed for you. I hope you like it." Stevie placed the crib in front of her. She got up to take a closer look, running her hand across the railing, she admired the smooth wood and how the pieces fit tightly together.

I laughed on the inside, personally admiring Stevie's own smoothness and the fact that he single handedly cured this woman of her sadness.

"Oh, Stevie. This is the most magnificent piece of furniture I have ever seen in my life." Avery went on and on about how remarkable it was.

His smile was outrageous. "Thank you, ma'am. I'm so glad you like it. I wanted to do something special for you during this great time of sorrow, something special for you and the little one." He nodded, his eyes sparkled in admiration of Avery.

"I really appreciate it and I know the baby will, too." She smiled. "You do such wonderful work, such a talented man, you are." She said.

"Thank you again, ma'am, building and fixing things is a

passion of mine, much more so since Cam here took me under his wing and gave me a place to live and repair on his behalf, allowing me to get sober and do something positive with my life." Stevie said.

Cam's eyes widened. We were both concerned that he may have revealed too much about himself.

"Well then, what a blessing Cam and Marry have been for the both of us." She said, unbothered by any past statements.

"Maybe one day if you're not busy, Ms. Avery, you would like to accompany me out to Cam's farmhouse and let me show you around the place, only if it's okay with Cam." Stevie said.

Cam agreed, then the two of us began to leave the room to allow Avery and Stevie some time alone. But before we could make our exit, Stevie began to make his.

"Since I travelled here by truck, I think I should head back. I'm quite tired." Stevie said.

Cam spoke up. "Hey Stevie, can I talk to you for a second?"

"Excuse me, miss." Stevie said, nodding to both Avery and me.

Stevie accompanied Cam down the hall and into his study. They shut the door behind them, but I knew what Cam was saying to Stevie. I knew what he was asking of him.

While they were gone - I admired the bed right along with Avery. I believe she was smitten by Stevie.

I finally heard the door open and the two of them emerged.

"Everything okay?" I asked Cam.

"Just fine, my dear. Stevie is going to be spending a couple of days with us if that's okay?" Cam said.

"Absolutely." That was an easy one.

Avery knew all about what happened with Sharon and Shelton and how Skylar was a product of their love affair.

She was also aware how Stevie became VAM. She didn't know about his addiction issues, but he disclosed that himself. There were no longer any secrets.

Wesley was back in Colorado and agreed with everything that was going on here in Charlotte. He also knew what Cam was going to ask of Stevie. There was a great reward awaiting Stevie.

Skylar, still bed ridden and unable to walk or fully take care of himself, needed a VAM - DNA Transplant. Cam was forced to ask Stevie for the favor. If everything went as planned, Cam intended on giving Stevie the deed to the farmhouse, under certain conditions of course.

"Stevie is willing to give Skylar the DNA that he needs to help him walk, be self-sufficient but most importantly, to live." Cam said.

Avery reached over and patted Stevie on the knee, proud of his noble gesture.

"Once the transplant is done, Stevie will completely heal in a day or two. He'll be as good as new. It will take Skylar quite a while longer to gain the strength he needs. During this process, we will add a few more staff members to assist Skylar on his journey.

"I am a little nervous, Cam." Stevie courageously told Cam.

"Don't worry Stevie, I will be right there with you." Avery said as she gently placed her hand on his. That was enough for any morsel of fear to leave Stevie's body.

"Ohhhhh, girl!" Rayan's voice echoed through the house as he began to sing, he and grandmother were still locked up in their room.

Cam and I just hung our heads and laughed. The expression on Avery's face was priceless and Stevie grinned, which was a welcome change from the fear he was once showing. Cameron began to kick and a lot. Leave it to Rayan to change everyone's mood in a split second.

Dr. Patak called for Stevie and Cam. There was no time

to waste, he was ready to proceed with the transplant, today.

"Stevie, I wouldn't do anything to hurt you." Cam spoke softly to Stevie as if he were a child. "Dr. Patak is the best in his field, I will be there through the whole thing as will Avery."

Stevie looked towards Avery and gave a slight smile.

"She'll nurse you back to health. Won't you, Avery?" Cam smiled in her direction, also.

"I promise." Avery winked.

"Okay. So, y'all are going to be there with me the whole time?" Stevie asked.

"Yes sir." Cam said.

Dr. Patak went on to tell Stevie it was a simple operation and only required a couple of needles and a scope or two. I could see Stevie's face begin to discolor. I hoped he didn't faint.

"I've had my fair share of needles, and I really don't like the idea of that, Cam." Stevie said.

Cam's eyes became red with anger, I knew his fangs were up next. He always acted like this when he didn't immediately get his way.

Stevie cut his eyes over to Avery who was now visibly shaking, fearful of Cam's change.

"Okay, do it right now and put me to sleep. I don't want to know that any of this is happening." Stevie said.

"That's a deal." Cam said in a growling, raspy tone before changing back into nice, human Cam.

Dr. Patak hit Stevie with a sedative so fast, none of us knew what happened when Cam jumped behind Stevie and caught him before he collapsed to the floor. Cam wrapped his arms around Stevie and guided him over to the gurney. Nurse Grace swung it around the corner, and they rolled him away to Skylar's room.

Dr. Patak's staff hurriedly brought in all the supplies he would need as Cam went in to explain the procedure to

Skylar. He told him his Uncle Stevie would give him part of himself like Wesley had done in the past, the only difference was guaranteed healing for Skylar. He would be as normal as any vampire around. I'm not sure what that says about this whole thing.

Cam no longer than got his last word out before Dr. Patak put Skylar to sleep. Dr. Patak explained the procedure would take three hours. Cam insisted on getting hourly updates to which the doctor agreed as if he had a choice.

Grandmother and Rayan were still in their room, unconcerned about what was going on out here in the real world.

Hour one: Everything was going as planned.

Hour two: Still perfect.

Hour three: Cam began to pace the floor.

"Come sit by me." I said as I patted the adjacent sofa cushion.

Avery sat across from us in complete silence.

Cam put his hand on my stomach and felt Cameron kicking. "I can't wait for our son to get here." Cam said.

I looked at him with admiration. He was my everything.

I leaned over and gently spoke into his ear "After Cameron's arrival, we can do this again if you want to. I love you Cam."

Cam's eyes turned the same bloody red as during his silent fit of anger towards Stevie. I watched as the little white parts of fang began to pop through his gums. I could feel myself blushing, embarrassed that Avery was witnessing his uncontrollable passion for me.

He bent to lift me from the sofa just as Skylar's door opened. Dr. Patak emerged, no longer wearing his hat or gloves. His presence prevented Cam from doing whatever he had in mind.

CHAPTER 26

Dr. Patak sat down across from the three of us. He lowered his head, folded his hands, and sighed deeply.

Cam growled in confusion.

"No, Cam." Dr. Patak quickly lifted his head back up. "Everything seems to have gone rather well. I will keep Skylar on a monitor for the next few days to be sure there won't be any side effects from the transplant." He began to stand.

"What about Stevie?" Avery hurriedly asked.

"Stevie did so magnificent that I almost failed to mention him." The bags under Dr. Patak's eyes showed clear exhaustion. "He's a lot healthier than any of you could imagine. I've cared for and examined many VAM vampires, but Stevie has something different than the others. I should get his approval before I disclose this medical information about him." Dr. Patak said.

"That won't be necessary." Cam now stood over the doctor. "You're on my payroll. Any knowledge you have about any vampire, or anything for that matter, belongs to me. Did you fail to read your contract, Dr. Patak?" Cam asked.

I turned my head so as not to look at anyone during this near heated conversation.

"Of course." Dr. Patak scoffed.

"At one point I thought Stevie's heart rate had increased and was beginning to beat out of rhythm but once I checked it, I knew that was not the case. I did a quick X-ray to confirm my suspicions and I was correct - Stevie has two hearts." Dr. Patak stood in silence for just a moment awaiting a response.

I gasped, Cam seemed unaffected, and Avery was amazed by the find.

"I have only seen this once before in a vampire and the species was none that I believe you are familiar with. I found this in a male Russian soldier during my internship in Ukraine. We can speak later. I must go check on my patients." Dr. Patak slowly walked back towards Skylar's room. He stopped abruptly, turning towards Avery. "Ms. Avery, a double heart is one of best things a vampire could possess, and it doesn't work out too badly for their mate, either." He winked.

"I think I'll go in there with him." Cam stood up.

"Don't do that." I pulled at his arm hoping he would sit back down. "You don't want to carry any germs into that sterile environment." I said.

"I suppose you're right, but I do need more information on Stevie's deformity." He laughed.

Avery rolled her eyes and let out a giggle.

"You know I'm kidding, right?" Cam asked Avery.

"Of course." She blushed.

"Rayan!" Cam belted out into the air. "Ray!" He yelled again and just like a bolt of lightning, Rayan now stood in front of us all, still in his boxer shorts. "You could have gotten dressed first, brother." Cam stared at Rayan's feet. "You need to do something about those dogs." Cam laughed.

"So, Dr. Patak says Stevie has two hearts and it's a good thing. Have you ever heard of such?" Cam said.

Rayan rubbed his chin, flopped down on the couch, and crossed his legs. "I have heard of this phenomenon once before. There's some entitlement that comes along with that from my understanding." Rayan said.

"Entitlement to what? Whatever do you mean?" Cam said.

"The second heart is given by the maker. Once he was bitten and changed into an immortal along with that came a certain amount of feeling. Those emotions of love were so deep in his maker that he secreted enough of the sentiment into his victim or creation, however you chose to look at it. That emission began to grow in Stevie to form his second heart which basically belongs to his maker." Rayan said.

I gasped at the thought.

Cam disappeared down the hall. We all got up and ran after him but not in time to prevent him from wrapping his hands around Dr. Patak's neck. He glared down upon the doctor who was dangling from his grip. "Does this mean Shelton lives in Stevie?" Cam hissed.

Dr. Patak reached upwards in an attempt for Cam to release him.

"Let him go!" I screamed. "You will never get your answers if you injure him. You need a vampire therapist!" I screamed before breaking down into tears. "You have anger issues, and I don't like it!"

"She's right brother." Rayan hovered next to Cam finally convincing him to put Dr. Patak down.

"I apologize, Dr. Patak." Cam said.

"It's okay." Dr. Patak accepted his attempt at being sorry, which I knew he was not.

"How much do they pay you for you to be okay with this type of treatment?" I now screamed at the doctor. Everyone ignored me.

"Can you please answer my question though, sir?" Cam politely asked Dr. Patak.

I stood in amazement waiting to hear how he would respond to Cam.

"Shelton does not live in Stevie. I know how Stevie and his sister, Sharon, were changed and I'm aware that Shelton had love for Sharon that surpasses a lot of people's understanding. So, when he came to the scene of the crash, his intentions were only to change Sharon - It would be my belief that he knew she would gain another heart from his bite but before he could do so, Read stepped in and took Sharon from him. I'm not sure how it happened but when he bit Stevie the passion that had already built up in his mouth like an organism - oozed out into Stevie and he received the second heart." Dr. Patak's pause from speaking became too long for Cam.

"Hurry it up, Patak. I don't have all day." Cam snipped.

"Only head vampires of certain circles have two hearts and know they can give their second heart to a forerunner – Someone they wish to take their place if they were to ever meet their final death. From all the things I've heard about Shelton, I think he was crooked all along and wanted to give the love of his life, Sharon, the second heart, so that in his absence the evil he was creating would never cease to exist. She would carry on the darkness he was creating." Dr. Patak said.

Cam kept his hands in his pockets to prevent himself from fidgeting or worse.

"The Russian vampire I told you about, his maker gave him the second heart because of his military intelligence and strength. He thought that giving him the heart would increase physical strength amongst his group to where they could withstand any army. But they didn't last that long, having set up their habitat in a Ukrainian forest called Cherkasy, the forest was set ablaze by their enemies and all the tree dwelling vampires succumbed to the flames. All Russian vampires are tree dwellers." Dr. Patak said. He washed his hands, dried them off and gave us a piece of advice.

"Don't forget that even in the world we live in, evil never wins. This is going to prove to be the perfect example." Dr. Patak laughed.

"With Shelton now dead, by VAM law and all rights given unto immortals, Stevie should be crowned head vampire. What Shelton meant to do here has backfired - With Stevie's demeanor and love for common folks, it's not in him to do bad to another being." Dr. Patak said.

After Dr. Patak spoke these words, his eyes widened as he looked around the room in expectation of something, but nothing happened.

"Welp, I think we need to bring Wesley in on this one."

Rayan said. "What has been said here today doesn't go any further than this room. We all need to be on the same page. Rest up, family. I believe we're all going to need it." Rayan left the room but immediately returned followed by Wesley.

"I'm here. Let's get this party started." Wesley was quite a jokester but even with his funny remarks, we knew he was always serious.

"Cam, let's you, me and Rayan take a walk to your study. I need a quick briefing on the situation we have here." Wesley was already walking away when Cam and Rayan got up to follow.

"Excuse me, my love." Cam bent down and kissed my forehead.

"Yes, he'll be back, my love." Wesley mocked him while laughing.

I decided to peek in on Skylar and Stevie, make sure they were doing okay, imagine my shock when I opened the door to find Avery and Stevie's lips locked so tightly that I wondered if they could breathe. I glanced over at Skylar who was still unconscious and quickly shut the door. I could feel my face heat up from embarrassment, thankfully neither of them realized my presence.

I grabbed a bag of jalapeno potato chips from the pantry and headed up to my room, at least there I couldn't bother anyone or so I thought. I cradled those salty treats like a newborn, grabbed the remote, flipped through the channels, repositioned myself again on the huge fluffy maternity pillow Cam had given me and then I felt it, water began to soak my clothing and the bed sheets.

I froze in fear, unsure of what had just happened. It became evident when the contractions started. I was in labor! It wasn't time yet. Dear Lord, please let my baby be alright. This was all happening way too quickly.

I tried to get up and go for help. My legs buckled underneath me, I screamed out in pain. I placed my hand over my stomach as a source of protection when I felt myself going down to the floor.

Cam appeared and scooped me up before I fell. He took me directly down to Dr. Patak. I wrapped my arms around his neck and began to sob.

"It's too soon." I moaned.

Wesley, Rayan, and grandmother flew in like giant hawks and stood over me, each now as vampires, fangs out, nails and claws visible and ears at attention. They panted heavily as they became fixated on my belly. I didn't fear any of them, I only feared the unknown.

The ultrasound equipment was quickly rolled over next to me. The nurse moved speedily to strap the heart monitor across my stomach. She then wiped my forehead with a wet cloth, calming me down.

Cam was now pacing and weeping. "My baby."

Dr. Patak asked everyone to leave the room while he performed the ultrasound to make sure baby Cameron was not in distress.

"That will not be necessary, please expect our presence through whatever procedures you will be performing on Marry including delivery if that shall also take place today." Wesley spoke with authority but remained calm.

The four of them didn't retreat back to human form as I assumed they would.

Grandmother peered over at Dr. Patak like a vulture ready to strike. Rayan motioned for her to come stand closer to him. She hissed at her husband. It was all quite comical had it not been so serious.

Dr. Patak didn't respond to Wesley in words, he simply reached over and flipped the light switch off, bringing a darkness upon the room. The glow from the ultrasound was the only light I could see.

"I never liked him anyways. He will be my first kill if my great grandchild is not perfect." Grandmother spatted off. Rayan shrilled loudly at my grandmother. She cut her eyes up towards the ceiling attempting to control herself.

The room quieted even more so than before.

"Mrs. Marry, Cam." Dr Patak said.

"It seems as though baby Cameron has grown too big for Marry to carry him any longer. He is absolutely ready to meet his mom and dad. His dimensions slightly exceed that of a baby carried to human term, his heartbeat is good and truthfully, I am beyond comfortable with delivering him today. I also deem it necessary.

"Patak, come speak with me in the hall." Wesley demanded.

Dr. Patak's face turned a pale white. "Wesley, I have everything under control." He whined.
Wesley surprisingly took that for an answer.

"How can this be?" I asked. "I'm only a little over six months now."

"The supernatural growth aspect comes from Cam's side of the family." Dr. Patak laughed, no one else found his remark funny.

"Your contractions will start to become more frequent, and the pain will worsen but, if need be, I can give you an epidural to help with the pain." Cam looked at me as if he disapproved. I don't know what he's thinking – My body, my choice.

"There is one thing that concerns me, the baby appears to be breech but we will try our best to turn him." Dr. Patak pressed play on a little C.D. player he had sitting in the corner. An upbeat catchy song began to play. "It's a proven fact, music will make babies turn quicker than anything." Dr. Patak said.

Hours went by, the contractions were almost unbearable. I wanted so badly to ask Dr. Patak for an epidural. Cam must've read my mind. He placed his body directly in front of me at the foot of the bed. He made eye contact with me. Neither one of us said a word, our eyes remained locked. The pain subsided.

Wesley, Rayan, and grandmother were still minding their posts. They hadn't budged even a centimeter.

Cam was now pacing back and forth wondering what was taking so long.

Rayan began to snap his fingers. Cam paused and looked at his brother out of the corner of his eyes. "Okay, I see what you're doing here." Cam laughed.

"If no one can hurry this up, his daddy can." Rayan smiled.

Cam joined in with the snapping and they both began to sing in sync. It wasn't long after that, Dr. Patak gave me instructions to push. "Push, Marry!" Dr. Patak's voice loudened. "Push! I see his head!" Dr. Patak said.

It was during that last push that I felt so much pain, I thought the child had to weigh at least twenty pounds. I wanted to yell out, not just from the pain but from this overwhelming feeling that I couldn't put a description on.

Dr. Patak continued instructing me. I could hear his voice and the deep breathing of every vampire around me.

"You're doing great!" Dr. Patak had the nurse move the incubator closer to my bedside. "One more time, sweet Marry." Dr. Patak said.

I gave it all I had.

"He's almost out!" Dr. Patak cheered me on. The pressure and pain didn't subside. I felt it more now than ever. I screamed in agony!

"Dear Lord!" Dr. Patak exclaimed. "There's another one and it's got a grip on Cameron's feet. It's coming out with him!" He nervously chuckled.

Cam's eyes widened, his face lit up and then he frowned, smiled again and lastly began to clap. "Marry, there is two!" Cam wiped the sweat from my forehead. As Cam's excitement increased, the sterner and more focused the rest of the family became.

"It's a girl! It's a little girl and she came into this world holding onto her brother! She will always have his six.

Hallelujah!" Dr. Patak was thrilled with the delivery of our babies.

Both babies were placed in my arms against my bare chest. Cam and I began to talk to them, telling them how much they are loved.

"Camille" I said. "We will call her Camille." She was a lot smaller than her brother.

Cam's bloody tears covered the floor, adding to the pool of red mess were the tears of Wesley, Rayan, and grandmother. None of them could hold back their emotions. Wesley excused himself from the room to regain his composure.

Come to find out, Wesley did have Patak put the second baby in me as a gift. Cam and I were now overjoyed with the idea of two babies. We were both relieved when Dr. Patak apologized for his recent bad attitude, citing the fear that Cam's second seed didn't take seeing as she was never visible on the ultrasound. She was always hiding behind her brother.

Wesley let out an ear piercing shrill from the hallway. We all paused for a moment of silence, realizing Wesley was having a multitude of emotions. Cam was the first vampire to father a human child.

Dr. Patak allowed Cam to do the honors of weighing in the babies. Cameron was a whopping nine pounds, twelve ounces and twenty-two inches long. Camille came into this world at only five pounds and eight ounces, seventeen inches long. She might've been itty bitty, but everyone knew she was already full of spunk. They both had a head full of jet-black hair just like their daddy and the most beautiful green eyes one could imagine. They gleamed like emeralds in the sun. Their little skin was pale, their lips were a ruby red and perfectly rounded. The most beautiful babies I had ever laid eyes on and not because they were mine.

Official birth certificates were made. The father was

listed as deceased. Cam hung his head, realizing that this world would never see him for who he truly was, he was nonexistent in this place.

"Grandmother, hold the babies, please." I said.

"Come to granny, you little sweeties." Grandmother took Cameron as Rayan reached for Camille.

I pulled Cam down closer to me and showered him with love and kisses. "You are everything and more to me and your children." I reassured him. I was thankful for Cam, my husband, and the father of my children.

"Wow, so you are going to let them call you granny?" I asked grandmother.

She winked at me.

"If she's grandmother then I cannot simply be Uncle Rayan." Rayan spoke up.

Cam laughed. "Okay, it's grandaddy then."

Rayan was ecstatic with the title.

"Wesley, what shall they call you? You are most certainly a father figure so you too shall be grandaddy, grandaddy Wesley." Cam said.

Wesley accepted the name and then excused himself to the hallway once more to shrill. Cameron formed his first smile to the sound of Wesley.

"Announce their full names." Grandmother insisted we introduce them properly.

Cam held our baby boy near his chest. "Please welcome into this crazy family, Cameron Marcel Rosenthal." Everyone cheered.

"And last but not least, a dear sweet surprise, Camille Marol Rosenthal." Cam said. The room cheered once more.

I fed the babies for the first time and then I rested.

As fate would have it, we did need both bassinets. Cam prepared the room for the three of us. We would join him there later this evening.

Stevie was moved into Avery's room. They sent their congratulations and love to us by Rayan. They would visit soon enough. The focus for them was Stevie's healing. They would be a complete family of their own whether they knew it or not.

Wesley sent word that Benji and Sarah would be headed our way in the next couple of days, both excited to meet the babies.

Read delivered a whole library of children's books to the twins but didn't stay long, citing business in the big city. We all knew better.

CHAPTER 27

I woke to find Cam feeding Cameron while Camille was fast asleep in her little bed.

"I see one of my sleeping beauties is awake." He smiled as he rocked back and forth gently humming to Cameron.

Camille spread her arms out and grunted. It appeared she was feeling around for her brother. She let out the most horrendous scream. She wasn't soothed until I placed her in Cam's other arm next to Cameron.

Cameron cried with his fierce tone once he realized the bottle had been removed from his mouth.

"I can't see how this boy is still hungry." Cam said.

We had a specially formulated milk for the babies, something Dr. Patak made in the lab. They loved every drop of it.

I offered Cam some sleep, figuring he had probably been up most of the night. He reassured me that he was well rested as were the babies who also slept all night. I supposed he had put some sort of Cam magic on them.

I felt absolutely no pain and was ready to jump right into motherhood. I wouldn't have believed in a million years that childbirth would be this easy.

Rarely did either of the babies' fuss. I couldn't have wished them to be any better. Cameron seemed to only cry when he was hungry and Camille, well, she would get mad when she wasn't close to her brother.

Sleeping in the bassinette's didn't last long. The only way Camille would sleep was if Cameron was next to her. We had to opt out for a larger store-bought crib.

I knew a lot of people would disagree with the babies sleeping in the same bed, but this situation was different, and it wasn't like I was going to blog about my journey with the twins or anything. My children were very well protected. There were things put in place by their father that would keep them out of harm's way. Things that no one could begin to understand except for this family.

"Marry." Sarah came running through the door. "So, I'm Aunt Sarah and this is Uncle Benji, right?" The first question out of her mouth.

"We wouldn't have it any other way." I said.

Sarah spoke the infamous baby talk to them, goo-ing and gah-ing. They loved every minute of it. When she finally laid them down, they kicked their little legs and squealed wanting more interaction with their Aunt Sarah.

I had to continuously wipe the slobber from Cameron's mouth. I ran my finger over his gums – top and bottom and I could have sworn it felt like he was already cutting teeth. It wouldn't surprise me, the way he stares at my food as if he could take a big bite. Camille couldn't care less if she ate just as long as her brother was right there with her and that she was the center of attention.

Once Sarah and Benji were gone Cam and I sat in the bed holding the babies, relaxing and just watching a little television. Life couldn't get any better.

"Oh dear, was that your stomach growling?" Cam laughed.

I immediately covered my stomach with the palm of my hand. My eyes widened when I admitted that I was starving.

"I will have one of the ladies prepare you something." Cam said.

"No, no, let me do it. I could stand to take a little walk through the house, alone." I cut my eyes over at him.

"As you wish." He now cradled both babies. "I'll just love on these two while you're gone."

I threw on my housecoat and bunny slippers and headed down the steps. The house was eerily quiet. The walk to the kitchen seemed abnormally long. I was almost at my destination when I was startled by a repeated clicking noise. I turned to see Skylar making his way towards me! He was using his walker and moving rather well.

"Skylar, what on earth are you doing?" I asked.

"I feel good, Marry! There was a little voice inside of me insisting that I get up and walk so, here I am." He let go of the walker and held his arms up for a brief second before he started to tumble over. I gasped, fearing a fall but he managed to use his upper body strength to prevent that from happening.

"Wow! Look at you! Let's get you in seat." I helped him to the table and encouraged him to rest before taking the trip back to his room. "Wait right here, I need to get Cam."

Skylar smiled in approval, happy to share his newfound movement with his Uncle Cam.

We left the babies in the bed; they curled up next to one another and snored rather loudly for such tiny little creatures. Cam looked back at his twins and smiled.

"I should have Dr. Patak meet us down there just to give Skylar a good looking over." Cam said.

I agreed, this happened so fast and was so new to us all.

Dr. Patak checked Skylar from head to toe, exclaimed it a miracle and described Skylar to be as healthy as Stevie before the surgery took place. "It's as if he's a brand-new VAM! No illness present! But you must still rest." Dr. Patak instructed Skylar back to bed.

"I'm feeling good. I want to stay here with my family. I've spent enough time in my room - in that bed!" Skylar argued back with him.

"Actually, I'm glad the boy has the strength to argue." Cam whispered in my ear. He was right.

Patak then raised his voice "Go!" He demanded, pointing down the hall. Skylar's fangs burst through his ruby red gums - That was a first. It was almost exciting even though I knew the unexpected was about to occur. His color changed but only slightly. His ears were cuter than Cam's when they developed. But his nails - They were longer than any I had ever seen. Cam grinned at the sight of them.

Patak's face dropped, his feet moved in place. He wanted to run but he couldn't. Skylar picked his walker up and slung it across the room.

"I quit, I quit. I am no longer employed here, Cam! You can just mail me my last paycheck." Patak screamed. "Matter of fact, keep it!"

"I don't think there's going to be a need for that, doc." Cam replied.

Skylar jumped on Dr. Patak and tore into his neck with his virgin fangs, he drank of him like a dehydrated man walking through a dessert in a hundred-degree weather in the midst of a sandstorm. I have seen this happen many times, but I have never seen a person's blood be taken from them at that magnitude. Dr. Patak's skin now looked like a piece of torn clothing lying on the floor.

"Cleanup crew!" Cam and I looked at each other and spoke in sync while smirking. However, this was no joking matter – Cam informed me that a boy must mind his manners and learn.

"Skylar, go to your room. You can't just do what you want when you want to. Now go! I will send someone in to clean you up!" Cam said.

"Marry, you go upstairs with the babies. I'll be up shortly." Cam said.

By the time help came for Skylar, he had already cleaned and dressed himself.

Cam ordered all the hospital equipment and beds out of our home. When the cleanup crew arrived to handle Patak's body, in addition to his skin and bones, they took everything associated with the doctor away.

Cam had a long talk with Skylar and told him there were rules to the vampire game and even though he was only part EVG, he was going to conduct himself as EVG while living under our roof.

Skylar understood and agreed. "I just want to be a regular boy, Uncle Cam." He said.

"You are a regular boy and one that's loved very much." Cam replied.

"When can I see my Uncle Stevie?" Skylar asked.

"Soon, real soon. Hopefully this evening or in the morning." Cam said.

Wesley sent word to Cam that since he was the one that helped Stevie get clean, he should also be the one to tell him about his inheritance, his new role as leader of VAM. Wesley had been in touch with the VAM council and made them aware of what was going on. They were quite shocked to learn the identity of the second heart recipient, but they all respected their code of ethics and agreed when Stevie was ready, he would be able to take his place back in their group and as their superior. They weren't in any rush for a leader right now since the council was able to dictate new rules and reprimand those who broke laws in his absence.

This was going to be interesting to say the least.

Cam still wanted to give Stevie the farmhouse for his hard work and dedication, not to mention the fact that he saved Skylar's life by bringing him to life even though the beginning was quite monstrous.

We told everyone that Dr. Patak retired his position after reaching his long-term goal of a successful double birth for a Human - Vampire couple.

I was glad my home was no longer being used as a hospital.

CHAPTER 28

Skylar was up and about doing normal boy things. His transformation was amazing.

We turned our focus to Stevie. His recovery was dragging, it was taking way too long for him to get his strength back.

Since Dr. Patak was gone, we reached out to another doctor and had him pay a visit to our home to evaluate Stevie. We probably should have done this way before now, but in true Stevie fashion, he kept insisting he would be fine.

Stevie had gotten up for a while, about a week ago, leading us to believe things were on the up and up. But now his color was beginning to diminish, and he was all but bed ridden. Avery stayed by his side every moment of every day. Her stomach was growing large, Cam decided to have her checked out also to make sure the baby was progressing as normal.

The twins were nearly a month old now. They were growing like little weeds, but Camille hadn't outgrown the need for her brother.

Everyone except for Wesley decided to stay here with us in Charlotte. He had gone back to Colorado.

"Cam, how soon can you get a doctor out here to check on Stevie?" I asked.

"Today. I've already made the call and he should be here shortly." He replied.

It wasn't long after, there was a knock at the door. It was our new physician. Cam introduced himself as this was the first time they met face to face. Dr. Alexander was a new hire but came highly recommended.

Cam reached out his hand to shake the doctor's. "Cam Rosenthal - Nice to meet you." He said.

"Chad Alexander - The pleasure is all mine." He was an older gentleman, probably in his late fifties, well-groomed and professional. He did, however, reach for a small bottle of hand sanitizer, squirting it into the palm of his hands, and then rubbing ferociously in circles. "Please don't mind me. I have a phobia of germs but know that will help me keep your family in tip top shape." He said nervously.

"Whatever works for you." Cam said as he turned around to show him the office he would be using during his stay.

"Thank you for accommodating me in such a short time. Mr. Rosenthal." Dr. Alexander said.

Cam smiled and asked him to meet him in the living area when he was ready to begin his rounds.

Here we go again - The same old hospital routine I had grown accustomed to and disliked so very much.

First stop would be to see Stevie.

"I have read the chart that Dr. Patak left behind and this is all so interesting. I don't know why we shouldn't be able to have him fixed up in no time. You all can come in with me or wait in the hall, whichever you feel most comfortable with." He said.

As to be expected, Cam and I went in with the doctor.

Avery sat in a chair by Stevie's bedside as it had become uncomfortable for her to stay in certain positions due to her size.

Stevie muttered something from his bed.

"What is it, Stevie?" Cam asked.

He spoke a little louder this time.

"Something ain't right with me, Cam. I feel it. I ain't ready to go yet. I finally have something to live for." Stevie looked in Avery's direction, tears welled in his eyes.

"Hey, buddy, you're not going to die. I promise you that, Stevie." Cam said, glaring at the doctor.

"No, you're surely not going to die." Dr. Alexander said as he began to put his stethoscope back in his pocket after checking the rate of Stevie's hearts.

"I haven't seen this before, but I have read a few articles

on the matter. That second heart needs to come out. It's obvious he's in love, true love. I hate to say it but that is what's causing the beat to be irregular and fast, taking all his strength away. He'll never get better unless it's removed." The Dr. explained.

"I know with that second heart comes a lot of responsibility. he will lose that once the removal is complete. The choices are slim at this point. Remove the heart - All is well or keep the heart and all the perks that come along with it and never be able to use them because you will be bedridden for seemingly ever." The doctor continued.

The look on Stevie's face said it all. No one had told him or Avery about the second heart pending his rehabilitation. She was as white as a ghost at this news also.

"Cam, did this man just say I had a whole 'nother heart?" Stevie asked.

Avery still looking on.

"Okay listen." Cam was talking fast. "When Shelton changed you, he injected his venom into you or whatever you want to call it. I call it venom because that dude was an absolute snake. It formed a second heart in you which he had hoped to give to your sister whom he loved as much as he could love anyone. He hoped the two of them could continue an evil vampire society and launder money or whatever else it entailed but Read bit her first and so ends the story. Oh, and you are leader of VAM right now because of the second heart. But it's killing you, so it's got to come out and you lose your rank. What do you want to do?" Cam said matter of factly.

"Take it out! I ain't never wanted to be no leader of nothing. I just want to be with Avery and live happy!" Stevie screamed.

"Done, my man." Cam patted Stevie on the shoulder.

"Doc, take it out. How long will it take him to heal afterwards?" Cam said.

"He should be up and about tomorrow if you want to remove it today. It's basically like taking a splinter out of a human's finger. I would only want him to rest a bit so the anesthesia would have ample time to wear off. I've seen people act wild after surgery from the medication so just to be on the safe side. Does that work for you Stevie?" The doctor asked.

"Yes, sir. It does." Stevie responded.

"Okay, I'm going to go check on the others and I will be back shortly to get that old splinter out of you." The doctor chuckled.

"I'll be right back. I'm going to go ask Rayan to contact Wesley so that we can set up a meeting with VAM. It's going to need to happen quickly - I'd say as soon as tomorrow. I have enough empathy for them that I don't want them to go leaderless, but I don't want Stevie's health harmed in any way either. So, this is the way things must go. In a few hours - They will most definitely be without a number one and I feel they need to know that." Cam said.

I wondered how the chain of command went for the VAM group. There was Shelton the leader – now deceased. Loren the second in command who moved to first after Shelton's death, but he too is now deceased. I wonder who was third? It appears Stevie trumped everyone with the leaders given heart but now with that being done away with - Would their council just be in command? That wouldn't seem right. What if they were ever in a disagreement? I can't see how that would work. Cam was right to get Wesley to call a meeting with everyone.

"Let me go see these precious babies you have told me about."

I had Dr. Alexander follow me to the steps that led to mine and Cam's suite. I took Camille from the nurse's arms and sent her away. Cam walked in behind us and picked up Cameron.

"Wesley's on his way and should arrive tonight by

plane. The VAM council is also headed to Charlotte in the wake of this unforeseen event and so neither party will have to worry about any threatening behaviors or retaliation, we have all agreed to meet at the farmhouse which is now considered neutral ground seeing as I have already signed the deed over to Stevie though he doesn't know that yet," Cam rocked Cameron back and forth.

Cam knew it would be hard to get Stevie to accept such a large gift but with his signature already placed on the document, there was nothing Stevie could do about it. The farmhouse was his.

"Dr. Alexander, these are the twins - Cameron and Camille." Cam introduced the doctor to the babies and vice versa which I found cute. They looked at the doctor and didn't bat an eye.

"They're stubborn." I laughed.

"May I hold one?" He asked.

"You should probably give him Cameron because Camille will scream bloody murder if he holds her." I said to Cam.

"She doesn't like to be held by anyone much, unless it's her daddy or myself and she won't lie down unless her brother is with her." I said.

"Sounds like a bit of separation anxiety. She'll probably grow out of it. I couldn't imagine being in the womb with someone for so long and then them not being there anymore. I don't see any problem with you allowing him in the crib with her if it makes her happy." Both babies smiled when he spoke those words.

"Ah - you understand what I'm saying - Do you little one's?" They smiled again at the doctor's comment.

"Mr. and Mrs. Rosenthal, I think we are dealing with some gifted children here. Let's set up monthly meetings so I can monitor their growth, both physical and mental. I think we have a couple of little Einstein's on our hands. They look perfect as of now, and I don't expect that will ever change." He said as he smiled at the babies again.

Cam had sort of a worried look on his face as he sat in the rocker listening to the doctor.

"Are you okay?" I asked him.

"I'm fine my dear - Just thinking." He replied. I knew he must've been worried about something because he never thinks that hard. I just didn't know if it was about Stevie's extraction or the meeting coming up.

I called for the nurse to come back up with the babies as Cam and I followed the doctor back to Stevie's room where he would perform his final exam, which was on Avery. After that would be Stevie's extraction.

Cam and I waited in the hall while he checked Avery. When he came out, he said everything was fine. It appeared the baby would arrive in a couple more months.

"Do you want to witness Stevie's immediate healing?" The doctor asked.

I guess we really didn't have a choice. We had brought Stevie into this and now, we would see him all the way through.

Cam and I entered the room and stood next to Stevie. I took his hand and told him everything would be okay.

"Look buddy, it's your time to shine. I know you've been down for a while now. But I believe this doctor here is going to make you a hundred percent better. Don't you worry about any of the other stuff either. Wesley, Rayan, and I are going to handle all of that. It'll be like none of this ever happened. Oh, and I got a surprise for you when you're back on your feet, tomorrow." Cam said.

"I sure hope I'm back on my feet tomorrow, Cam. I just really don't think I can take too much more of this." Stevie said.

Avery didn't know what was going on around her. She was over in the corner fast asleep. That baby was draining all her energy. Oh, how well I knew that feeling.

Dr. Alexander administered Stevie a sedative and waited

about five minutes for him to appear comatose. He then took a Heart removal kit off the medical tray. I didn't even know there was such a thing. I thought he was joking when he told us earlier that it would be as easy as removing a splinter but what he had was so similar to the little contraption used to remove splinters that I almost couldn't believe my eyes. It was larger but the same, watching him perform the removal made it clear the concept was identical.

"Marry, if you get sick easily - you may not want to watch this." Dr. Alexander said.

Luckily, I had never been the one to get queasy at the sight of anything gruesome.

He dug the heart removal device under Stevie's skin and pulled it right out just like a splinter! It was amazing. He didn't have to stitch him up or anything. His body immediately healed, naturally.

Dr. Alexander placed a warm cloth over Stevie's skin where the incision was made and fifteen minutes later, it was as if nothing ever happened, no scar, not anything,

Stevie woke up soon after that. He rested for the remainder of the day and was out of bed by morning.

"Good morning, love." Cam leaned over me in the bed and placed a gentle kiss upon my lips. He whispered so not to wake the babies.

"We're headed to the old farmhouse to meet with the VAM council members." He said.

He left me with an uneasy feeling. I was worried to say the least.

Once the three of them left, I went to get my grandmother, leaving the babies with the nurse. I told her exactly how I felt. She made the decision that the two of us were going to sneak to the farmhouse. I wasn't sure if that was such a good idea, but she insisted that we should protect our husbands at all costs.

"Grandmother, I have babies and I am not even

immortal. I don't see how this could possibly be a good idea." I said.

"Don't be such a wuss, Marry. The babies are asleep, they have caretakers. We will come straight back home as soon as we see that everything is kosher."

I decided I should have kept my mouth shut but it was too late for that.

"You drive, Marry, let's take your Benz since it's black. Less likely to be noticed." She said. I pulled the car around to the front and she got in. We were both now wearing all black jogging suits. I felt ridiculous.

The ride there was a silent one until we neared the turn.

"What's the plan?" I asked.

"Okay, about a couple of hundred feet before we get to the driveway, turn the lights out - then park underneath that big tree by the pond. We'll walk up to the house by keeping close to the fence line. Once we see inside the house, we will be able to tell which room they are in simply by the lights. We'll go to the window and peep through - hopefully we can hear what they are saying. Simple as that."

I scoffed though I guess it was as good a plan as any. I couldn't believe I let her get me into this. Cam will have a nervous breakdown if he sees us.

We made it to the tree and did exactly what she described. The kitchen light was visible. We headed that way, ducking down close to the ground like we were in the armed forces. I had to talk to myself to keep from laughing.

We approached the window, dropped down further, and leaned our backs against the house. I could hear them talking. Thank goodness because I don't know what Plan B would have consisted of.

Grandmother, requiring a little more than the words we could hear insisted that I turn around and peek into the window.

"No!" I was getting excited but still trying to talk to her

in just a whisper.

"I want to know how many of them there are, Marry. They will not see you - now just slowly raise yourself up and look." She wouldn't take no for an answer.

I turned and faced the house - put my hands on the wood siding and slowly moved up to where my eyes were barely over the window seal.

"Do you see them? How many are there? Are there any women in there?" She said.

"No, be quiet. There's five VAM, Wesley, Rayan, and Cam. No women, grandmother!"

"That's good then, if need be, we can go five on five." Grandmother said as if we were at a battle royale.

The men sat around a round table. Cam was facing the kitchen sink and for a second there, I thought he could see me. I fell back to the ground and told my grandmother to shut up. I felt like she was about to get us caught.

"Just listen, seeing them is not going to help us. We need to hear what they are saying." I said.

She scowled at me but for once decided to take my advice.

The voice I could now hear was not one that I recognized. I knew it was a VAM speaking.

"Listen, so we don't miss out on anything." I said.

"We have all talked and agree that we could compensate you by giving you fifty percent of the money we are sure that Shelton obtained illegally." An older VAM spoke, I could tell his seniority by the gruffness in his voice.

"That's not necessary but I will allow you to donate that fifty percent to the Children's Hospital in Memphis as it deems beneficial for all of us and should we make the agreement at hand then no one - not a single immortal from either group will ever lack anything and will be well taken care of, medically. We have our hands in many ventures." Wesley said.

My Grandmother smacked my arm like I didn't just hear

what they had said. "A merger? Marry, are they trying to merge. I don't know how I feel about this." She said.

"More is better than less and if you put the top two groups together then you can never fall victim to any of these other common vampires." I told her.

"Wait, listen. What did he just say?" I missed the last statement from VAM because Elizabeth over there was breathing too hard. I guess she called herself getting mad at the conversation they were having.

"He said the only thing they would ask of EVG is fairness and equality of all vampires. They want to change the name to EVAM!" I said.

Grandmother began to squirm, loudly moving around.

"Stop! I'm not trying to be disrespectful but please stop!"

That didn't help. Grandmother started pouting.

"They're getting up from the table! We need to make a run for it." I said.

"No, wait a minute more and see what their final comments are." She again was bossing me around.

"Wesley, we know that you will be an excellent leader. This group has been through so much and we really need someone behind us who will push us to our true excellency. I believe wholeheartedly that we will be better together. Cam, Rayan - The pleasure has been all ours."

Their chairs scraped against the floor as they all stood up to shake hands.

"Good night, gentleman. We will meet in a couple of days after my lawyer has drawn up the documents, to review and sign." Wesley said.

"Run!" Grandmother said. We took off like two bats out of hades and made it back to the car safely. I burnt rubber speeding out of there. We had to make it back home before they did. I parked the car quickly back in its spot and we hurried in, changed clothes, and placed ourselves in one of our normal spots. We both jumped in our beds, pretending to be asleep.

I heard the front door close. It sounded like Wesley, Rayan and Cam were all three happy about the decisions made tonight.

I personally didn't see anything wrong with it.

I heard Cam walk up the steps, so I rolled over on my side and closed my eyes. I felt his presence beside me. He was breathing as hard as my grandmother was at the farmhouse.

"Marry… Marry…" He placed his hand on my shoulder and gently shook me. "Did you not think I would see you at that farmhouse tonight?" He said. His voice was harsh and reprimanding.

I continued my act of sleeping.

"Do you really think that I don't know what my wife is doing at all times? Haven't we had this discussion before?" He said.

I felt him crawl into the bed next to me and slip under the covers. His breath was heavy and hot upon my neck. He then whispered in my ear "Then you know I think it's beyond attractive when my wife does things that could be deemed harmful to make sure her husband is alright."

I turned and looked at him and the kiss we shared at that moment was more intense than any I could remember. He moved my hair and drank my blood.

"Change me! Change me!" I screamed. My stomach was full of butterflies almost like the first time we kissed. The look on his face made me think that he was going to, but he didn't.

We both laughed after little giggles from Cameron and Camille filled the room.

"It just feels like they know way too much to be so little." I said.

CHAPTER 29

Cam knocked on Stevie's door.

"Come in." He hollered out.

He was as good as new, packing to head back to the farmhouse. "Avery's coming with me, Cam. We're going back to the farmhouse." Stevie looked Cam directly in the eyes.

"I hate to see y'all leave but I really need my space back." Cam laughed.

We all laughed.

"Stevie, I have something for you and I'm letting you know now that you cannot refuse my gift. Do you understand? Trust me, you don't want to fight with a vampire of my caliber. This is no joke." Cam kept a serious face.

Cam took the deed for the farmhouse from inside his coat pocket. "The farmhouse is yours." Cam said. "Man, you've done a lot for Skylar, and for yourself by getting clean and staying that way. You are now about to start a family with this wonderful woman. I applaud that. It takes a real man to do what you did, and I want you to be rewarded for that. So, the farmhouse and all the land that it sits on belongs to you. Plus, I told you already you can't stay here." Cam joked, trying to keep from tearing up.

Stevie's eyes welled with blood, he grabbed Cam and hugged him. Cam's shirt caught the tears. Cam bugged his eyes over at me where Stevie or Avery couldn't see his expression. When Stevie finally let go of Cam, Stevie walked towards me with his arms wide.

"Nah, not her. I'll hug her for you later." Cam said.

I blushed; my face heated up.

"Cam, I don't mean to sound ungrateful because the Good Lord knows I am beyond thankful, but I was wondering something and you can tell me no if you think it's a bad idea." Stevie said.

"What?" Cam snapped unsure of the question.

"Avery and I was wondering since you and Mrs. Marry got the twins and a lot on your hands, once we get back down to the farmhouse and settled in and once I'm able to set up a room that's at least equal to the one you have for him, can my nephew, Skylar come live with us? Don't get mad, Cam. I'm just asking." Stevie said quickly.

Cam's face lost all expression. I was worried about what would come next.

"Show me that room and we'll talk about it but if I do decide to let you take Skylar, you need to understand all major decisions for him will still be made by me." He was very stern with his words.

"Yes sir, Cam. Yes sir." Stevie said.

Cam had given Stevie more hope. I didn't think the idea was too bad, after all Stevie is Skylar's biological uncle and he is the reason the boy is still alive.

Stevie toted all their luggage in one arm and Avery with the other.

We said our goodbyes.

It was only a little over two weeks when Stevie came calling for Cam to view the room he created for Skylar.

Cam wasn't in a hurry to see what we already knew would be a masterpiece. He realized that once we took the trip to the outskirts of town that Skylar would no longer live in our home with us. I tried to encourage him to see the positive side of things, but he viewed it as a loss.

He finally concluded that it might be fun to take the twins out for a spell. They were going on two months old and had not been on their first car ride yet.

So, to the farmhouse, we would all go.

Cam pulled the Cadillac SUV around to the front of the house. Since Skylar was going along for the ride, we needed the extra room. We wanted him to feel secure in any decisions made on his behalf. I felt in my heart that Skylar would choose Stevie and that would be okay.

Cam placed the car seats in the vehicle.

Cameron cried all the way to the car but was fine once the door shut. Camille reacted the same as her brother. Skylar slid past Cameron and sat in between the babies. I taught Skylar to use the seatbelt almost forgetting he, too, had never been on a car ride. That made me want to make sure Cameron and Camille learned everything about all things. I wanted them to be book savvy and of course have common sense. I prayed that they would be diverse, kind and loving to everyone. I also needed them to know the difference between good and bad people. The real world is full of both and the bad pretend to be otherwise.

We turned out on the street and immediately Skylar started to pick at Cameron. Okay, I thought, he hasn't had much experience if any with babies. So, I warned him. "Skylar, he's a baby, you can't pick at him and make faces, you will scare him."

Skylar burst into tears.

"Sweetie, I'm sorry. I was just telling you. I'm not mad at you." I said.

Cam looked into the rearview mirror and had this huge grin on his face.

Skylar was trying to say something but all I could hear was "Not you, Marry. No. Him. He." Skylar didn't speak another word all the way to the farmhouse.

I pretended to smack Cam on the leg. "Why are you laughing?" I said under my breath.

"Oh, nothing, my dear. Boys will be boys." He said. He turned the radio up and we began singing along with the oldies.

A faint whining noise continued from behind me.

"Skylar, what's wrong? Are you okay?" I said.

He wouldn't respond. I contemplated whether or not he was just scared of being in a car. Cam was able to ignore his pouting. I, on the other hand, had a hard time with it. My own babies didn't act like that, and they were tiny.

Maybe Skylar should stay with Stevie.

I was overjoyed when we pulled up to the farmhouse.

Skylar jumped out of the car and ran towards Stevie as soon as we came to a complete stop. The physical healing that had taken place within him was extraordinary. I marveled at his ability to get from point A to point B in a matter of single digit seconds.

"Uncle Stevie, Uncle Stevie! I want to live with you and Avery. I'm never going back to Uncle Cam's house. Those babies are mean to me." Skylar said. He nearly jumped into Stevie's arms.

"That's ridiculous." I said.

We all laughed at the thought of the babies being mean to Skylar.

"Kids, these days. They'll say anything to get their way." Cam said. He oddly stared Skylar directly in the eyes.

"You haven't even seen your room yet, nephew." Stevie said.

We followed Stevie into the house. Avery was lying on the couch, her feet propped up to help with the swelling. I knew the miserable feeling.

"It won't be long now." I smiled while bouncing Camille up and down on my hip.

"I hope not. I'm so ready for my body to get back to normal." Avery smiled.

"Keep me posted." I told her as we walked down the hall to what would soon be Skylar's room soon, a lot sooner than we expected.

"Wow." Cam and I were both blown away when we walked into the room. Stevie had worked his carpentry magic once again. He turned the back bedroom into what appeared to be a Pirate ship. Skylar's bed was nestled on the ship's deck with a place to put his television and gaming equipment.

I handed Camille to Cam and let him hold both babies while I went and checked everything out for myself.

"Stevie, this is nothing short of miraculous." I climbed aboard the ship. "When the twins get older you will have to design their rooms for us." Cam agreed it was the most magnificent thing he had seen for a boy Skylar's age.

"Can I stay now? Uncle Stevie, can I please stay now?" Skylar begged Stevie.

"Skylar, don't you want to go back with us and pack all of your things?" Cam said, appearing to agree with him staying.

"Can someone back at the house pack it up, please?" He continued pleading, now with Cam.

"You're a persistent little somebody." Cam laughed. "I'll bring the necessities and once all of your things are together, I'll make a second trip later this week." Cam said.

"Stevie, you take care of my boy. You hear me?" Cam said.

"Of course, Cam, I will never let anything happen to Skylar. I promise you that." Stevie replied.

"Now go on over there and hug your Uncle Cam, Aunt Marry, and the babies before they leave." Stevie instructed Skylar.

He hugged Cam and I and then he lightly patted the babies. As soon as his hand touched them, they started screaming bloody murder. I imagined their faces would be soaking wet from the tears but, no, they were bone dry.

We said our goodbyes. The trip home was pleasant, I guess it did us all some good to get out and Skylar was now in bliss with his Uncle Stevie.

Rayan and grandmother sat on the couch like two hawks waiting for our return. "Where have you been?" They both stood up, each taking a baby.

Cam and I threw our hands up.

"So, we should tell you before we go anywhere?" Cam said.

"With our grandchildren? Yes!" They shouted.

Cam rolled his eyes, the rest of us laughed.

Cam took Skylar his things later that evening and when he returned home, he had brought with him a dozen red roses just for me.

"What's the occasion?" I asked.

"You are forever my Blood Queen, right?" He asked.

It was a nice gesture but in a creepy way. I had never thought of myself as a Blood Queen. I tried to be funny by saying "Blood Princess, maybe."

"Come on now Marry, you can't be the Blood Princess. Camille is the Blood Princess." I figured he was saying all of this for fun.

"Thank you, my Blood King, for the beautiful red roses. They are reminiscent of your lips, blood drenched and luscious." I played along as if this were a game.

His fangs became immediately visible. The babies were still with Rayan and grandmother giving Cam I had a chance to role play or so I thought.

CHAPTER 30

The past few months had been peaceful. VAM and EVG decided not to merge but formed a very strong alliance with one another. They included Wesley, Cam, and Rayan in an interviewing process where they would choose one vampire from the council to take over their lead position. It was a unanimous vote, and everyone agreed that the eldest of the five should become their number one. He was a rather ancient vampire named Tressell. He was outspoken and preferred right over wrong. Even though Wesley had chosen not to be their leader, Tressell still gave half of the ill obtained monies to the Children's Research Hospital in Memphis as gratitude for his patience and help in their trying time.

Stevie was added as the fifth council member after Tressell took his place as top authority. They wanted someone fresh and young to help with the group.

Avery and Stevie got married. They had a small ceremony in Charlotte with all of us present. Skylar walked Avery down the aisle but still wouldn't make eye contact with the twins. He referred to Stevie and Avery as mom and dad now. They had become a very happy and sweet little family - Whom were all thrilled with their new addition. Avery gave birth to a baby boy about three months ago. He wasn't nearly as big as Cameron when he was born but he was a pretty good size. She and I already had plans that our sons would grow up to be the best of friends. They named him Lorenso to show respect for his lost vampire father, Loren. Lorenso was like the twins in the way that he was all human though made from a vampire seed.

Cameron and Camille toddled around everywhere. They acted as if they owned the place, which if it were told, they probably did. They were the apples of their daddies' eyes. He couldn't be prouder, and neither could I.

Camille was still her brother's shadow. Her pale white skin, dark colored hair, and ruby red lips made her the most beautiful little girl ever. She was quick on her feet, too. If she didn't want to be caught, there was no catching her.

Both babies had a mean streak; it would be a lie if I told you otherwise.

Cam and I both found ourselves excited for Christmas this year - Having the twins gave Cam a new title. We were going to call him Saint Nick but decided to stick with Santa. I have a feeling, he was never much of a saint.

The day after Thanksgiving, we put up a Christmas tree just like regular human families. We even celebrated Turkey Day this year with all the family, fun and laughs. We were thankful to be together, we just didn't have the traditional feast.

We danced around and sang Christmas carols while putting up the Tanenbaum which is German for Fir tree. I try and teach the twins any and everything I can.

"What's wrong Sarah? I grabbed her by the shoulders trying to get her to calm down. I thought something tragic had occurred.

She bounced up and down screaming and crying, Cam turned vampire ready to avenge her until she managed to hold her dainty hand up in the air and show off the huge diamond engagement ring Benji gifted her with.

Wesley got up and left the room, we were all pretty sure it was to cry. Wesley's baby girl wasn't much of a baby anymore. Thank goodness about a half hour later we heard the shrill of approval coming from somewhere deep in the woods. We all breathed a sigh of relief.

For the next couple of weeks, we wrapped presents for the three babies and Skylar. Christmas cheer was everywhere.

Along with that major diamond ring Benji bought Sarah, he also gave her a professional grade camera. She had always loved the arts, every sort.

Cam and I took the babies to buy matching outfits and the two of us found the exact sweater in both male and female.

Since the babies were the first of their kind, we decided to have Sarah take our photograph in front of the Christmas tree so that we could send out Christmas cards to all the Elite Vampire Group and even VAM.

She loved the idea as much as we did.

She decided that I should hold Cameron and Cam should hold Camille. So, we could do the daddy, daughter and mommy, son thing. We were all in place and ready for the photo shoot to begin.

She took a couple of great pictures to start with but then I felt myself becoming dizzy.

"Those are beautiful, but I need to take a break. I'm feeling a little lightheaded." I said.

I thought about going to lay down for a moment, but my mind blurred even more to the point I couldn't remember what it was I needed to do. I started to ask Sarah if we could reschedule when I heard Cameron and Camille speak their first little words right as the camera snapped and a bright flash ensued.

"Momma - love." They said in sync.

Cam moved closer to me as if he knew I was about to pass out.

I looked at my two babies and both had grown little fangs, they hung uncontrollably over their bottom lips. Drool was everywhere. I leaned down to wipe their mouths thinking I was hallucinating. The closer I got to them, the closer they moved towards me. Cameron sunk his fangs into the right side of my neck. Camille leaned over from the grip of her father's arms and put her fangs deep into the left side of my neck. Cam's grip on her became loosened, he began to drop her when he realized what was going on. Sarah let her camera fall to the floor and grabbed both babies.

Their bites were more ferocious than I could have ever imagined. The pain was indescribable,
and I knew I was dying when I felt the warm blood running down my body. I was falling in and out of consciousness.

Cam picked me up in his arms and carried me to our room. He apologized over and over again, swearing that he did not know.

"Marry, I had my suspicions, but I promise you that I didn't know they were vampires. I love you, Marry! Please don't leave me. Please don't leave us! I will do anything – Anything!" His voice was getting louder and louder.

I knew exactly what this was - We would never be broken.

And now I knew the answer to the question I had asked myself repeatedly from the time Cam asked me to marry him.

As we made our way up the steps, I had just enough strength to whisper to him. "I will die with you - so that we can always be forever."

He fed me his blood and now I am what I thought my children were not. I am what my family chose for me. I am immortal because of my children. A forever love is never broken.

THE END.